APPALOOSA

SUMMER

By

TUDOR ROBINS

Island Trilogy – Book One

Library and Archives Canada Cataloguing In Publication Data

Robins, Tudor, 1972 –
Appaloosa Summer / Tudor Robins

Paperback.
ISBN 978-0-9936837-0-1

Editor: Hilary Smith
Proof-reader: Gillian Campbell
Cover photograph: Kacy Hurlbert Todd / Boss Mare Photography
Front cover design: Allie Gerlach
Spine / back cover / interior design: Cheryl Perez www.yourepublished.com
Website: Lynn Jatania / Sweet Smart Designs
Author photo: Debora Dekok

Tudor Robins gratefully acknowledges the financial support of the City of Ottawa.

Also by Tudor Robins

Objects in Mirror

To Tim, Evan, and Bryn,

for believing in my writing

Chapter One

I'm staring down a line of jumps that should scare my brand-new show breeches right off me.

But it doesn't. Major and I know our jobs here. His is to read the combination, determine the perfect take-off spot, and adjust his stride accordingly. Mine is to stay out of his way, and let him jump.

We hit the first jump just right. He clears it with an effortless arc, and all I have to do is go through my mental checklist. *Heels down. Back straight. Follow his mouth.*

"Good boy, Major." One ear flicks halfway back to acknowledge my comment, but not enough to make him lose focus. A strong, easy stride to jump two, and he's up, working for both of us, holding me perfectly balanced as we fly through the air.

He lands with extra momentum; normal at the end of a long, straight line. He self-corrects, shifting his weight back over his hocks. Next will come the surge from his muscled hind end; powering us both up, and over, the final tall vertical.

It doesn't come, though. How can it not? "Come on!" I cluck, scuff my heels along his side. No response from my rock solid jumper.

The rails are right in front of us, but I have no horsepower – nothing – under me. By the time I think of going for my stick, it's too late. We slam into several closely spaced rails topping a solid gate. *Oh God. Oh no. Be ready, be ready, be ready.* But how? There's no good way. There are poles everywhere, and leather tangling, and dirt. In my eyes, in my nose, in my mouth.

There's no sound from my horse. Is he as winded as me? I can't speak, or yell, or scream. *Major?* Is that him on my leg? Is that why it's numb? People come, kneel around me. I can't see past them. I can't sit up. My ears rush and my head spins. *I'm going to throw up.* "I'm going to…"

****

I flush the toilet. Swish out my mouth. Avoid looking in the mirror. Light hurts, my reflection hurts, everything hurts at this point in the afternoon, when the headache builds to its peak.

Why me?

I've never lost anybody close to me. My grandpa died before I was born, and my widowed grandma's still going strong at ninety-four. She has an eighty-nine-year-old boyfriend. They go to the racetrack; play the slots.

If I had to predict who would die first in my life, I would never, in a million years, have guessed it would be my fit, strong, seven-year-old thoroughbred.

Never.

But he did.

Thinking about it just sharpens the headache, so I press a towel against my face, blink into the soft fluffiness.

"Are you OK?" Slate's voice comes through the door. With my mom and dad at work, Slate's been the one to spend the last three days distracting me when I'm awake, and waking me up whenever I get into a sound sleep. Or that's what it feels like.

"Fine." I push the bathroom door open.

"Puke?"

I nod. Stupid move. It hurts. Whisper instead. "Yes."

"Well, that's a big improvement. Just the once today."

She follows me back to my room. She's not a pillow-plumper or quilt-smoother – I have to struggle into my rumpled bed – but it's nice to have her around. "I'm glad you're here, Slatey." I sniffle, and taste salt in the back of my throat.

I'm close to tears all the time these days. "Normal," the doctor said. Apparently tears aren't unreasonable after suffering a knock to the head hard enough to split my helmet in two, with my horse dropping stone cold dead underneath me in the show ring. I'm still sick of crying, though. And puking, too.

"Don't be stupid, Meg; being here is heaven. My mom and Agate are going completely over the top organizing Aggie's sweet sixteen. There are party planning boards everywhere, and her dance friends are always over giggling about it too."

"Just as long as it's not about me. I don't want to owe you."

"'Course not; you're not *that* great of a best friend."

The way I know I've fallen asleep again, is that Slate is shaking me awake. Again.

"Huh?" I open one eye. Squinting. The sunlight doesn't hurt. In fact, it feels kind of nice. I open both eyes.

"Craig's here."

I struggle to get my elbows under me, and the shot of pain to my head tells me I've moved too fast.

"Craig?"

She's nodding, eyes wide.

"Like *our* Craig?"

"Uh-huh."

First my mom canceled her business trip scheduled for the day after the accident; now our eighty-dollar-an-hour, Level Three riding coach is *at my house*. "Are you sure I'm not dying, and you just haven't told me?"

"I was wondering the same thing."

"What am I wearing?" I blink at cropped yoga pants and a t-shirt I got in a 10K race pack. It doesn't really matter – I've never seen Craig when I'm not wearing breeches and boots; never seen, or even imagined him in the city – changing clothes is hardly going to make a difference.

Slate leads the way down the stairs, through the hallway and into the kitchen, where Craig's shifting from foot to foot, reading the calendar on the fridge. He must be bored if he wants the details of my dad's Open Houses, my mom's travel itinerary.

"Smoking," Slate whispers just before Craig turns to me. And, technically, she's right. His eyes are just the right shade of emerald, surrounded by lashes long enough to be appealing, while stopping short of girly. His cheekbones are high and pronounced, just like his jawbone. And his broad, tan shoulders, and the narrow hips holding up his broken-in jeans are the natural trademarks of somebody who works hard – mostly outside – for a living.

But he's our riding coach. Craig, and our fifty-five year old obese vice-principal (with halitosis), are the two men in the world Slate won't flirt with. I don't flirt with him, mostly because I've never met a guy I like more than my horse. *Major* ...

"Hey Meg." Craig's quiet voice is a first. The gentle hug. He steps back, eyes searching my head. "Do you have a bump?"

I take a deep breath and throw my shoulders back. "Nope." Knock my knuckles on my temple. "All the damage is internal."

Craig's brow furrows. "Meg, you can tell me how you really feel." *No I can't.* Of course I can't. Even if I could explain the emptiness of losing my three-hour-a-day, seven-day-a-week companion, the guilt at "saving" him from the racetrack only to kill him in the jumper ring, and the take-it-or-leave-it feeling I have about showing again, none of that is conversation for a sunny springtime afternoon.

Still, I can offer a bit of show and tell. "I have tonnes of bruises. And I've puked every day so far. And, this is weird but, look." I use my index finger to push my earlobe forward. "My earring caught on something and tore right through."

The colour drains from Craig's face, and now I think *he* might puke.

"Meg!" Slate pokes me in the back. "Sit down with Craig and I'll make tea."

Craig pulls something out of his pocket, places it on the table. A brass plate reading "Major". The one from his stall door. "We have the rest of his things in the tack room. We put them all together for you."

Yeah, because you wanted to rent out the stall. I can't blame him. There's a massive waiting list to train with Craig. And my horse had the consideration to die right at the beginning of the show season. Some new boarder had her summer dream come true.

I reach out; turn the plaque around to face me. Craig's trained me too well – tears in one of his lessons result in a dismissal from the ring – so now, even with a concussion, I can't cry in front of him. *Deep breath.* I rub my thumb over the engraved letters M-A-J-O-R. "There was nothing that horse couldn't do."

Craig sighs. "You're right. He was one in a million. Have you thought about replacing him?"

Chapter Two

A week passes in a strange limbo. I'm mostly better – but if I try to read for more than a couple of minutes, my lurking headache presses back in, so no school yet. I don't feel nauseous, but when I take our dog Chester out, and run to catch up with him, I'm left doubled over and dizzy.

I appreciate it when Slate comes to see me after riding on Wednesday. While Chester's delighted to have me home, I'm not sure talking to a dog all day is great for my mental health.

The day's warm, breezy; perfect for riding. "How was it?" I ask.

"Good, OK, fine."

"You don't have to hold back for me, you know. You can tell me it was great."

"Oh, my-one-and-only-Meg, I would tell you if it was great. It wasn't. It was fine. It'll only be great when you're back."

Every single day I'm tempted to go back, but then I imagine being a sad, sort of shadow person drifting around aimlessly. A rider without a horse. Until I'm well enough to ride, I don't belong at the barn.

I deflect. "Tell me the barn gossip."

"Um, well, there are two new grey ponies – one's an uber-expensive boarder, and one's a new pony Craig bought for the school – and you can't tell them apart. To the point where some intermediate rider rode the boarder's pony by mistake, and Craig only figured it out halfway through the lesson, when the school pony stuck his head over the field gate and whinnied.

Oh, and the new wash stall is ready, and the barn cat had kittens, and Major's stall is filled."

"Major's stall?"

She puts her hand on my shoulder. "Is that OK, Meggie? I thought if I said it fast, with everything else, it might be better."

I think for a minute. I didn't realize how much the spectre of that gaping empty stall was bothering me – how, when I thought of the barn, it was all I could picture. Now, Slate's removed it. I take a deep breath. "You know what? It *is* OK. It's fine. And, I'm going to the doctor's tomorrow morning. If he says I can ride, I'll come out with you in the afternoon."

"You will?"

"I will."

It doesn't feel like ten days have passed. The drive to the barn feels just the same. The tires hum on the highway, roll on the pavement of the concession road, crunch as gravel takes over. We pass through dense trees, then move into open farmland bounded with barbed wire, and finally hit the neat white wooden fences marking the edge of Craig's property.

Slate's in the backseat beside me, just like she has been so many times over the years, and, as usual, our helmets are tumbled on the seat between us. The difference is, where hers is scuffed and scratched, mine's brand-new; without a mark on it – "It's a welcome-back-to-riding gift," Slate told me as she handed it over. "Plus, you'd probably get lice if you borrow one from the schooling stash."

Another change; instead of waving and driving away when we reach the barn, my mom steps out and stretches.

"Emily!" Craig is grace and charm to the moms – the cheque-payers. He air kisses my mother. "It's been too long."

"Meg said you came to visit. I'm sorry I missed you; meetings, you know. It was so kind of you to drive all the way into the city when you're so busy."

"It was the least I could do ..."

While they chat, and while Slate puts on her half-chaps with the fiddly zippers that take forever, I turn away and walk to the barn. If I want to be alone when I see Major's stall with a new horse in it, I need to move fast.

I throw my shoulders back, take a deep breath, and step into the filtered light of the aisle. Blink twice, sneeze at the dust motes floating through the air, and turn left, to walk the twenty steps to the most familiar box stall in the stable.

The words are right there, on the tip of my tongue: "Hey Buddy." It's a phrase I've spoken hundreds of times over the last two years. But, at the last minute, I change them for "Hey Sweetie." Because the delicate head poking over the half door, with its bright long-lashed eyes, and near-perfect star, has to belong to a mare.

I step back to read her nameplate. "Little Rich Girl". So, yes, a mare.

She reaches her nose out, snuffles around my shoulders and face. She's gentle, her muzzle like moleskin, whiskers carefully trimmed. Groomed for the show ring. Which, of course, she would be. People don't pay Craig's prices unless they intend to compete.

She rests her face flat against my breastbone, and I reach to scratch behind her ears. She exhales a long, shuddering breath, warm and soft against my t-shirt.

I smooth a rogue chunk of mane to the left side of her neck. "This is a good stall. You'll like it here." I waited months for this stall to come free for Major. I wanted the internal window for him; the one where the barn cat sits and cleans her paws. I wanted him to have cross ties right outside his door so he'd never be bored. I've mucked this stall out for him, groomed him in this stall and, once, at the end of a very long day, fell asleep slumped in the corner of this stall while I waited for Major to finish the bran mash I'd made for him.

It's not Major's stall any more. A tear plunks on the mare's bright chestnut face and I blink to stop any more from falling.

"You OK?" Craig's at the far end of the aisle.

"Uh-huh." I whisk my thumb over the drop; press it into nothing more than a dark spot among the surrounding hairs. By the time Craig reaches my side, it's disappeared.

"I wanted you to know it all went OK with the ... uh ... *arrangements* ... for Major."

"Oh. Thanks. It felt like the right thing to do." It felt like a surreal thing to do, actually, when I was presented with the option of donating Major's body to a nearby big cat sanctuary. "Because he died without being euthanized, it would be safe for the cats," the vet explained.

For the cats to *eat*, she meant. Weird at first, but burying, or cremating something as big as a horse is more complicated than you might think, and the idea of having him rendered into glue was awful. By comparison, nature taking its course – some carnivores eating a herbivore – seemed much better.

The hunk of Major's mane sitting in my bedside table – the one I grabbed when he went down, and I fell off – is more important than his flesh and muscle.

Craig clears his throat. "I was wondering if you'd like to ride Apollo?"

Craig's warmblood jumper, imported from Europe; so expensive he's owned by a syndicate.

"I'd have to be worse than concussed to say no to that."

His brow furrows. "You are OK, right? It's safe to ride?"

"The doctor cleared me this morning. As long as I don't jump."

I don't tell Craig about the doctor's wagging finger, and his deep sigh, and his warning, "This is against my better judgment."

Craig beams. "Great! I'll pull his tack out for you."

As I grab a lead shank, and go to get Apollo out of his rubber-padded stall, there's something else I'm not telling Craig either. How can I explain that I feel only flat indifference about riding his super-star horse that's worth about five times more than any other I've ever been on?

I'm sure it will change once I get in the saddle.

****

Apollo feels like the sixty-thousand dollars he's rumoured to have cost. Where Major was whippy, stringy, this horse is rock hard everywhere: under my legs as I squeeze him, under my hands as I stroke his neck. It's like riding one big muscle. He punches the ground in his walk, and his trot nearly launches me out of the saddle with each stride.

Craig wanders in, coffee in hand, sips and watches, sips and watches. "What do you think?"

I'm glad he's not asking what I *feel* – my heart is refusing to lift, even though I want it to. But what I *think* is easy: "I think amazing. Powerful."

"That, and lazy, too. Come on, chase him up; he's barely moving." Then, in a tone I'm not used to, rushes to add, "If you're tired, or your head hurts, you tell me, and we'll take a break." He swivels to Slate; sounds more like himself. "Not you. You haven't been working that horse enough lately. No breaks."

But my head doesn't hurt, and I don't get tired. Or feel like crying. Or feel anything. Most every ride on Major gave me a moment of joy. Of pride. Like when he was just learning to do flying changes, and he unexpectedly threw one in for me in the middle of a course. "He changed for you!" Slate yelled, and my heart swelled. He loved me. I loved him. Life was great.

Or when we'd stand, and watch another rider do her course, and Major would turn and rest his nose on the toe of my paddock boot, and sigh. *Love.*

Those feelings aren't with me on Apollo, but at least being on horseback – even though it's not my horse – gives me a one-hour vacation. A mental shut off. All that matters is my legs, and seat, and back and hands. Everything I do is a communication. Apollo may be expensive, but he's a horse like every other horse. He talks to me with the swivel of his ears, his mouthing of the bit.

Once we've gotten to know each other, I tighten my legs, and relax my hips, and hold the reins as steadily as I can, and he lunges into an extended trot, hooves flying, reaching, all the upward, saddle-thrusting, motion focused forward, neck arched and mouth listening to my hands. I feel like I'm sitting on a charging bull, and I feel like I'm holding a carton of eggs in my hands, at exactly the same time.

"Beautiful!" Craig's nodding. "See that, Slate? She's not fiddling with his mouth to get the frame. She's driving from behind." He watches as we round the ring one more time. "That's enough. I want to see a nice walk transition, then give him a long rein."

Apollo stretches his neck long and low, his muzzle almost brushing the ground, demonstrating to Craig that he was working the right muscles, showing he's happy and relaxed. I rub his withers. "Good boy."

He is a good boy. He's a lovely boy. And I've been privileged to ride him – I know that. This ride has been like coming halfway home. Like when we flew back from England, and I was so excited to land in Toronto. It felt great, it felt like home. Almost. But it was only when we started seeing signs for Kingston and Ottawa on the 401 that the real feeling of home – of belonging – seeped into me.

Apollo's helped me back to my country, but my hometown's still out of reach.

"He's beautiful." My mom wasn't in the ring – in the magic oval – so for the last hour I've forgotten about her.

However, the fact that she's stayed for my ride – and that she's been watching instead of working – worries me. My mom never wastes her time, so if she's chosen to spend her time watching me, there's got to be a reason.

Eventually I'll find out what it is, so for now I just agree with her. "He's a great horse."

"What's that?" says Craig.

"I said he's a great horse."

"He is. And he went well for you. I was telling your mom you can ride him from now on if you like."

My mom turns to me, eyebrows raised, voice pitched high. "Isn't that a wonderful offer, Meg?"

"Well, Craig will take it back if I don't cool him out properly." It's only a temporary dodge, but it works for now.

Craig laughs. "You're right; keep him moving."

I circle around to walk Apollo next to Slate and her horse, Obsidian.

Slate reaches out to poke me with her dressage whip. "See that, Slate? See how perfect Meg is? Even with a concussion she rides ten times better than you …"

"Shut up."

"Why should I?"

"He's just being nice to me because I'm damaged goods, and my horse is dead. He'll go back to tearing strips off me in a couple of weeks. Let me enjoy it for now."

She shrugs. "You're right. Your hair looks like hell, and he didn't even give you crap for not wearing a hairnet. I guess he is going easy on you."

"Thanks Slate."

"Anytime Bestie."

****

Slate sticks her head back in the car after she steps out onto her driveway. "Walk the dogs?"

"Um, sure."

My mom twists around in the front seat. "You're not too tired, Meg?"

"No. I'm good." I look at Slate. "You take longer than me – when do you want to meet?"

"Half an hour?"

I raise my eyebrows. "You'll be ready?"

"Yeah, well, you'll have to deal with the flat-haired, non-made-up me."

"Good thing you'll be walking Garnet; I might not recognize you."

Twenty-five minutes later, flat-haired and non-made-up (but that's nothing new for me), I reach down and click Chester free from his leash. He immediately leaves the mowed path to bound through the wild grasses, already higher than my knees. The scope he gets – nearly straight up from a stand still – makes me shake my head. What could he jump if he was a horse?

As I watch, he's side-swiped by Garnet. Our families got these two dogs just weeks apart, and though now they're both settled – and, on their own, sometimes lazy – together they always revert to puppy ways.

"To the beach?" Slate is anything but flat-haired.

"How do you do it?" I pick up a hank of my après-riding hair, let it fall back in place.

"Oh the wonders of dry shampoo, my friend. I'll give you some for your birthday."

It's one of those early June nights, when the air is skin temperature – so light you can't even feel it. When minus-thirty January deep freezes, and sticky plus-thirty July blasts, are equally impossible to imagine. It's the kind of night you could declare perfect and nobody would argue.

We walk along the shore of the river, and when we get to a spot where the dogs like to splash out on the broad, flat rocks we stop, and sit on a fallen tree and stare over at the Gatineau Hills.

Slate clears her throat. *Here it comes.* "Hey Meg, you're holding your breath. What's up with that?"

"You're going to tell me something I don't want to hear."

"What makes you think that?"

"You never, ever, want to walk the dogs after riding. Never. You want to eat popcorn, and paint your nails, and watch back seasons of ANTM."

She spreads her fingers in front of her, studies her nails – shiny, but chipped – and sighs. "You're right. I don't want to have to tell you this now. After everything. But you're going to find out …"

Chester pushes his wet nose into my hand, and I close my fingers around his muzzle. "Just tell me."

"I … we … Obsidian is for sale."

"What?" My fingers scratch behind Chester's ear a little too hard, and he whines and ducks away. "But he's amazing. He's great. He's the perfect horse."

"I know. That's the point. It's the right time to sell him. He's at his peak. Somebody will buy him, and do well on him, and love him."

"I thought that person was you."

Slate shakes her head. "I get that it's hard for you to understand, Meg, but I'm done. I've had enough. I know it sounds stupid, and shallow, but I'm tired of driving out to the barn. I'm sick of getting dirty, and breaking my nails, and always having helmet hair ... God, it sounds pathetic, but just the fact that I notice all those things tells me I'm not into it enough anymore."

Not into it anymore. Her words run a shiver through me. I talk to cover it up. "But we were going to show all summer."

She nods. "And we would have. It would have been fun. But now it would just be me. And then I started figuring out how many shows I'd miss at the end of the season, anyway – to go to London..."

Ah, yes. University. Slate's a year ahead of me. And more brilliant than her hair-clothing-make-up-ANTM fixation would have you believe. She has an entrance scholarship to Western in September.

"I get it."

"You do?"

"I guess. I wondered what you were going to do. I never thought you'd take Sid to London."

"No, and there's no point in him sitting here, doing nothing."

"I get it."

She reaches over, squeezes my arm, right above my wrist. "There's one caveat to this, Meg. If you want Sid – if you want to ride him, and show him this summer – just say the word. He's yours. I've already talked about it with my parents. We'll sell him in September, after the championships, if that's what you want."

"It's an amazing offer, Slate …" I stand, stretch, snap my fingers for Chester. "Let's head back. I'm kind of tired."

"Oh God, your head. I'm sorry. Let's go." We're mostly quiet on the way back, but it's not because my head hurts. It's more because my mind won't stop.

Major is gone. And soon Obsidian will be too. I glance sideways at Slate. Suddenly even her departure, which has seemed far off for so long, feels imminent.

Everything's changing.

I could get my old life back. At least part of it. I've got lots of time to heal before the show season gets into full swing. I've been offered rides on my coach's Olympic-calibre event horse. My best friend has presented me with the option of showing her trained-to-the-eyeballs A-Circuit jumper. I could clean up this year; do even better than I could have done on Major.

But …

"What's that thing you always say when Ben's being an ass, and you decide you should definitely break up with him, and then you take his call, and fifteen minutes later you two are back together again?"

Slate raises her eyebrows. "Always?"

"More than once. More than twice. Would you prefer 'Often?'

She laughs. "OK, you're right." She claps her hand over her chest. "The heart wants what it wants."

The heart wants what it wants. Something in the pit of my stomach does a flip every time I hear that quote. Even when it jusapplies to Slate talking about her high school boyfriend.

Especially in the context of me thinking of the gangly, dirty, off-the-track-thoroughbred who stole my heart two years ago, and kept it as we grew and improved together. As he learned not to bolt, and I learned not to panic, and we went from the pair who were hard to get into the ring (Major knocked down more than one whipper-in during our early show days), to the pair who were tough to beat.

I don't know what my heart wants but, from the absence of any flip or flutter in my stomach or elsewhere, I know it's not showing Apollo or Obsidian.

If a persistent ache counts for anything, I'd say my heart wants things to go back to the way they were before Major died.

I guess just because the heart wants what it wants, doesn't mean it can have it.

Chapter Three

Slate: Ready Meg-O? Back to school … pick you up 8:45.
Me: Thx. See you then.

I'm up too early. I forgot to reset my alarm, which is programmed to give me time for a before-school run. I'm not quite there yet, though. Better to see how my head feels after a day in class.

So, a good forty-five minutes earlier than I need to be, I'm down in the kitchen, showered and dressed, opening and closing cupboard doors, staring at cereal boxes, wondering if I should use the time to make pancakes, and getting between my mother and her laptop one too many times.

She bumps into me as she turns from the coffee maker to her laptop, which has a place in every room in the house. Here, in the kitchen, it snugs in beside the fruit bowl. "For God's sake, Meg. What are you doing?"

"I'm, uh, making oatmeal, I guess." I fill the kettle and switch it on.

"So, how bad is it?" I should be used to it, but it still catches me off guard when my mom picks up conversations seemingly out of nowhere on her headset. The coffee's at peak percolation and the kettle's heading to the boil. My mom wrinkles her nose. "Excuse me, Miranda. Let me just get somewhere quieter. It's like a zoo in here. Now, you were saying ..."

I plunk a teabag into my mug, and green tendrils swirl out as I pour the boiling water over it. *Crap.* Not enough water left for my oatmeal. I refill the kettle and start again.

I tap my feet. Wait for the tea to steep. Drum the countertop. Wait for the kettle to boil.

Bing.

My mom has an email. What a shock. My eyes slide to the screen. Not one, but six new messages have piled up bold and important in her inbox since I last saw her check it five minutes ago.

The kettle clicks off and I turn away, just as something catches my eye. **Meg.**

I step back. Squint at the screen. **Re: Question about Meg.**

It's my mom's email.

But it's about me.

The sender's name washes a wave of memories through me. *South Shore B&B.*

Long grasses. Huge skies. The ever-moving St. Lawrence river. Gravel roads. Cows. The bakery, the general store, the village. The ferry.

Our island cottage.

The B&B beside it. Nearly a kilometre away by the long driveways and concession road; a third of that distance on the path mowed through the hayfield between the two properties.

Owned by Betsy and Carl.

Betsy, baking the best cookies in the world; carrying them out to the deck for me to devour with my big brother, Cam.

Cam and I always starving from building forts in the weeping willows, and from long "wild turkey hunts" led by Carl.

Carl, showing us how to build a bonfire; loading us up with buckets of corn to throw to the ducks in the pond.

The kettle's gone quiet and is going cold. My finger hovers over the touch pad. One click will tell me what question Betsy and Carl have about me.

My mom has the right to privacy.

I have the right to know what's being said about me.

I hold my breath, cross my fingers and *click*.

Scroll past the top threads:

Betsy: We understand, thanks for replying so quickly.

My mother: It's an interesting offer Betsy. But given the current circumstances, I don't think the time is right ...

To the original:

Hi Emily,

I hope this finds you well. It feels like much too long since we've seen you, and we're looking forward to the summer when we hope you'll be around more.

Speaking of the summer, Carl and I have a question for you. It's more a question for Meg, I suppose, but we thought we should run it by you first.

The B&B is getting so busy we didn't have a moment to ourselves last summer. As the weather is getting warmer, and our bookings are picking up again, Carl and I are remembering how much hard work it was. We got talking about it last night and were wondering if Meg would be interested in working for us this summer?

Of course, we know you and Jack would have to OK it first, which is why I'm contacting you. It goes without saying we'd keep an eye out for her, and pay her fairly, and maybe even give her some time off!

Let us know what you think and when we might expect to see you. Drinks on the deck?

Take care,

Betsy

A job. I've never had one. *The cottage.* It's been ages since we've gone – between my parents' work, and my showing, and Cam, who graduated from Queen's, to move onto McGill – there just hasn't been the time, or the reason, to drive to Kingston and the nearby cottage.

So, do I want it? A job? The cottage?

I know what I *do* want. The chance to decide for myself.

My mom's footsteps approach. The loose floorboard in the hallway creaks. My heart double-thumps, and there's a flutter in my throat. But I don't close the message. Don't click out of her email program. I stand my ground and I wait.

The best defence is a good offense. It was my lawyer-mother herself who taught me that. So, before she can register my nosiness; before she can call me on it, I'm on her. "Were you ever going to tell me about this?"

"Excuse me?"

"This message from Betsy." I peer at the screen. "Which first came three days ago. And, which, it appears, you've already answered on my behalf, without asking me."

"The message was to *me*, Meg."

"About *me*."

She walks to her laptop. Clicks out of the message, out of her email. Closes the lid. Stands as straight as she can. "I'm your mother."

"Yeah, mother. Not boss."

"Whoa, girls. What's going on in here?" My dad heads straight for the cupboard which contains his coffee flask. Picks it up and turns to the coffee maker. "Well?" His eyebrows are high as he lifts the carafe from the burner. "Emily?"

"Meg has been reading my personal email."

"Betsy offered me a job and *she* turned it down without even asking me."

My dad sets his flask down, stares at me. "And, just who is 'she?'"

Shit. I should have known he'd take her side. "Sorry. *Mom*."

"Apologize to your mother."

I move my eyes to her without changing my stance, or my expression. "I'm sorry I called you 'she.'"

My mom nods. Allows a tiny smile to turn up the corners of her mouth before pushing it down. "Apology accepted." She reaches for her coffee mug.

"So, what's this about a job?" my dad asks.

My mom's hand stops just shy of the handle.

I jump in. "Betsy and Carl need help at the B&B. I don't know all the details because I never got to read the email ..." *Don't look at her. Don't make it worse.* "... but they'll pay me."

"Hmmm. It might be good for you to have a job."

"Jack!" The word starts shrill, before my mom pulls her voice back down. It's a well-known fact that my mom gets to make ninety-eight per cent of the decisions, but when my dad decides to weigh in the other two per cent of the time, watch out. My mom has to tread carefully here if she wants to keep this particular decision in ninety-eight per cent territory. "I understand where you're coming from, Jack, but there are other considerations. We should probably talk about it."

He checks his watch. This conversation has already put him three minutes behind schedule. "Fine. Tonight, then."

A "bye" for me, and a peck on the cheek for my mom, and he's out the door.

"Good morning Mr. Traherne!" Oh, thank God for Slate.

I abandon my never-filled bowl, and cooled-down kettle. Grab a banana from the fruit bowl. Mutter "Better go," without meeting my mom's eyes, and I'm out on the porch in the fresh spring air in no time.

"You good?" Slate asks. "OK with going to school?"

"Oh yeah. I'm ready. It's time."

Chapter Four

My dad doesn't forget like I thought he would. Like my mom probably hoped he would.

Instead he comes home with research; print-outs of studies that show kids who have part-time jobs in high school are more independent, successful, entrepreneurial.

"Where on earth did you get these, Jack?"

"You're not the only one who can do research, Emily." His voice is mild, but it has the same firmness I've heard him use when explaining to a prospective home-buyer that no, they can't have a fully-treed private lot, and still be in walking distance to three coffee shops and a pub.

My mom's eyes flash. She literally rolls up her sleeves.

"Jack, I would be very happy for Meg to get a job – a part-time job, that fits around her riding schedule. Craig says Meg is very talented. So talented that he offered her a chance to ride Apollo. He says, on the right horse, she could make it to the Royal this fall."

"Does Meg even want to ride Apollo? Is Meg interested in going to the Royal? Meg just lost her horse in a showing accident. Maybe Meg would like a break." Since my dad doesn't even look at me as he asks, I'm assuming he doesn't want me to answer. Turns out I'm right. "Listen, Emily, Ian Millar is nearly seventy and he's one of the best riders in the world; it's not like Meg's going to run out of time."

The score is one-all. Which means we need to keep going.

"Meg gave up tennis, and soccer, and everything else, for riding. And we've invested so much time and money into her riding and showing. How can we just walk away now?"

My dad nods, as though to thank her for proving his point. "Exactly! Meg's riding has been so expensive. It would be nice to have Meg earn some money, for a change, instead of us forking out even more."

Two-two. Next round.

My mom sweeps her arm in my direction, but doesn't break her eye contact with my dad. "How can we let a sixteen-year-old live on an island, in the country, with no car, for ten weeks?"

My dad makes a little tsking noise, like this one is just too easy. "It's not like we're dumping her on a deserted island all by herself. Betsy and Carl are shouting distance away. They'll watch her."

It was close. I have to agree with my dad that it wasn't my mom's best argument, but she's hanging on. Tied at three, and we keep going.

"Can Meg even look after the cottage properly?" There's a quiver in my mom's voice as she launches into this one. "It's an *investment*, Jack. We paid all that money to have the floors refinished. If she leaves even one window open during a rainstorm, you know how the wind will blow the water in ..."

With this argument my dad's head starts shaking. He's the real estate agent, but he's not buying her property value argument. "Meg is perfectly capable of closing windows, and mowing the lawn, and doing the dishes. What's the point of having a cottage if nobody's allowed to use it?"

All three of us know my mom's beaten. If I had a trophy, I'd hand it to my dad. He's not done, though. "I had to work hard for everything I got. I started delivering papers at nine, and I've worked ever since. It was good for me; it'll be good for her."

My mom doesn't shake his hand, but she might as well. She signals her defeat by silently piling the dinner dishes in front of her, shaking her head, and standing to carry them to the counter.

"You'll have a great summer, Meg." My dad squeezes my shoulder, pushes back from the table, and heads upstairs to change for his evening tennis game.

I gulp. My breath shallows and quickens. *I'm going. Oh. My. God. I'm really going.*

I started this, not because I desperately wanted to go to the island; more because I was angry at my mom for not telling me about Betsy's email. *Be careful what you wish for.*

There's no way I can stay home now. The only thing my mom would hate more than losing this argument, is finding out she lost it for nothing – that I don't even want to go.

What do I have to keep me here, anyway? Slate's quitting riding, so if I show, it will be alone. And if I can't get excited about showing Apollo, what horse would excite me?

My mom wouldn't let me bum around the house all day so I'd have to find a job. Doing what? Serving coffee? Selling something door-to-door?

The cottage is beautiful, and Betsy and Carl are great, and I'll miss Major the same amount here, or there, and I can bring his hunk of mane with me ... so, yes! I'm going!

The first flutter I've felt since Major died, ripples through my stomach. It might not be pure joy, or excitement – it might be tinged with nervousness – but it's a real, actual, feeling, and it's gripping me, and I'm glad to be having it.

Chapter Five

I'm sitting crossways in the backseat of our car, legs propped on my duffle bag – stuffed with running gear and swimsuit (my priorities), a single summer dress (at Slate's insistence) and, at the last minute, riding helmet and half chaps (*just in case*) – jammed in the foot well. Chester's sprawled across the seat next to me, panting in anticipation of a good romp through the island fields.

Every now and then the bottom drops out of my stomach. Like when my mom asks "Do you have everything?" and I say yes, but my mind cartwheels over all the things I might have forgotten, and then it's too late anyway because we're already out of the driveway and heading down the street.

I shove my hand into the pocket of my shorts and feel the only thing I can't replace; the braid I made from Major's hair; a braiding band holding it in place at each end. I put it there, so it would be close to me; so I'd remember to find a safe place for it in the cottage.

Once on the island, our car whizzes effortlessly past a red-faced woman standing on her pedals, trying to push her bike along the highway's long, persistent incline, and I think *from now on that's me*.

Then, when we get to the spot on the road into the cottage where the trees narrow in around the gravel, and there's a little rise so you can't see ahead, and it's picturesque but also just ever-so-slightly mysterious, I think *every night this will be between me and the highway*.

But mostly I do fine. I push these thoughts away. I ask myself what's the alternative, and know there isn't one, because whatever my heart wants, it isn't to replace Major as though nothing ever happened, and it isn't a summer in the sweltering city getting under my mother's feet.

So I sit back, and take in the sweeping island skies, the rolling island fields, and the wildlife from soaring hawks, to swooping swallows, to awkward and clueless wild turkeys.

When we turn onto the long cottage driveway, the gravel rattles and pings under the car like it always does, and the long grasses and wildflowers whisper as they brush the doors and windows.

As the low, wind and storm-weathered cottage comes into view, my mom says, "Oh good, it's still standing!" and my dad says, "Looks like I'll need to mow the grass."

My gaze flicks past the cottage and the lawn. I squint to find the sturdy little apple tree I planted a few years ago, just barely poking a few budding branches above the field flowers, and scour the fields for the familiar deer that always uses our land as her nursery.

Everything's normal, except in two days, when my parents get back in the car to go catch the ferry off the island, I'll be staying here. Alone.

Chester reminds me of priorities with a whine and a nudge of his wet nose. I let him out of the car – watching as, with two leaps he's swallowed by the deep grasses – then start shuttling bags and bins and boxes out of the car and into the cottage.

The sky sears blue, without a cloud in sight, which is lucky for me since this is my only chance to enjoy the cottage before I go "on-duty." Carl and Betsy are taking the weekend as *their* last chance to visit their grandchildren before the busy summer tourist season starts, so my training begins first thing Monday morning.

I stay outside as much as I can. I read on the swimming raft, row across the bay to tiny Duck Island, and explore the fields with Chester where, together, we find the deer's newest fawn, white-dappled and craftily camouflaged in the filtered light falling through the branches of a huge weeping willow.

When I get too close to the cottage — when I let down my guard to tell my parents about the fawn — my mom swoops in. "Come with me, Meg. I have a few things to show you."

I sigh, and my dad raises his eyebrows, but jerks his chin after her retreating figure. "You'd better go. Just humour her."

I trail her through the cottage.

"You need to remember not to overload the washing machine, and only do laundry during off-peak times. The chart's here, on the machine."

I nod. "OK."

"Rinse down the shower every time you use it, and you won't have so much build up to worry about when you clean it."

Why would I use the shower when the river's out there?
"Sure."

"And these windows …" She turns to catch me rolling my eyes at the ceiling. "I mean it, Meg! It may be a joke to you, but it wasn't cheap to have these floors finished. If water gets in, and sits, it can ruin the windowsill, the wall, the floor."

"I know, Mom. I understand."

"I'm not so sure, Meg. I don't think either you, or your father, understand. I work hard to look after this place. I don't want anything to happen to it."

The shush of the sliding screen door interrupts her. "She gets it, Emily. She's a smart girl. We all appreciate how nicely you keep the house and the cottage." My dad puts his arm around my mom, and gives her a squeeze. "Now, let's go get some ice cream."

The sun blazing in the window wakes me early on Sunday morning, but when I pad down the stairs, the table's already set, the coffee maker, kettle, and toaster are on, and my mom's standing at the stove.

"Nice of you to finally get up."

I squint at the clock. "It's seven-fifteen."

"What's that supposed to mean?"

My dad calls through the screen door. "I need to show Meg something on the lawn mower."

"Fine!" My mom waves her spatula at me. "I'll just stay here and cook by myself. You'd better go."

I'm still tired. A yawn grips me as I join my dad on the deck, and follow him down the stairs and onto the lawn. "God, Dad, what do you guys want from me? I should have just stayed in bed …"

"Nothing."

"What do you mean, nothing?"

"I don't want to show you anything on the lawn mower."

"Then what?"

"I want to have a smooth morning. A good transition. I want your mother to leave here happy, and I want you to stay behind happy."

"Oh."

"Do you want that too?"

"I … yes … sure."

"Then just go along with her. Whatever she asks, say yes. It's for a couple of hours. Then you're free."

I rub my eyes. Look at my dad. Nod. "OK. Fine."

"She's only being snarky because she's going to miss you."

"She's going to miss the cottage. She's afraid it will never be perfect again."

My dad smiles. "She's going to miss you *and* the cottage. It's doubly hard for her."

"Whatever you say." My bare feet are soaked with dew. They leave dark footprints on the stairs as I head back up.

"And, Meg?"

I turn back to my dad. "Yes?"

"She's making poached eggs. What do you think of poached eggs?"

I swallow against the gag that instantly forms in my throat. Smile wide, with teeth. "I. Love. Them."

"Thatta girl."

I eat a poached egg peacefully, if not enthusiastically, and don't argue when my mom says she's going to give the cottage a good cleaning before she goes, and shoos my dad and I outside.

I'm halfway up the driveway, checking to see if the foxes have any kits this year, when Carl and Betsy drive by up on the road; home from their trip. I wave, they beep and a shiver goes up my spine. *Soon; I'll be working soon.*

Not long after, my parents' visit is done too. It's like watching a video playing backwards. Chester appears from a part in the grasses, and takes two leaps into the back seat. My mom rolls down her window. "Take care of yourself." I can't help but think she really means 'Take care of my cottage.'

The car rumbles away down the driveway in a cloud of dust and bouncing gravel, and it's quiet, quiet, quiet until the birdsong starts up again, and the bullfrogs begin banjoing, and the world along the banks of the river swings back into motion.

Everything moving, except me. Standing. Completely and totally by myself. *Alone.*

Then "Halloo!" yells Carl from his position halfway down the path mowed between the hayfield that separates our cottage from the B&B.

"Betsy made too much for dinner!" he calls. "Would you like to help us eat it?"

I thrust both my thumbs high in the air above my head where he can see them.

"Great!" He holds his own thumb up. "Come up whenever you're ready!"

****

As soon as Betsy sees me, she grabs me in a hug, murmurs over my shoulder, "We were so sorry to hear about your accident." Then steps back; holds me at arm's length to ask, "Are you sure you're OK?"

I thought I was done with tears, but there's a warning sting in my eyes. I blink, hard, and bite my lip. "I'm fine."

"But you must miss him. Remember that time we came to your show and he stole that little girl's cotton candy and had pink foam coming out of his mouth?"

The noise I make is half-laugh, half-sob. The memory is sharp and sweet. "I do. But I'm here now, and that's good."

"Of course. If you ever want to talk, we can, but for now, I think we should eat."

Betsy is an out-of-this-world cook, and we eat at Carl and Betsy's round kitchen table – made from the same rough barn board that's all through our cottage – and watch the sun set over gold-tinged fields that run down to the St. Lawrence shipping channel.

With my accident out of the way, we're free to talk about lighter topics. Carl and Betsy make me laugh with the story of their grandchildren filling up the furnace outlet pipe with decorative river rock. With the contractor scheduled to come on Monday to replace the pipe for eight hundred dollars, Carl got out a Shop Vac and sucked all the rocks out but one.

They tell me how every night they went to sleep in the guest room alone, and woke up with three kids, two cats, and a dog in their bed.

Carl interrupts when Betsy starts another story and says, "Maybe Meg would like to know about working in the B&B?" And

Betsy looks at him, and me, and says, "Meg is smart, and we'll be patient, and everything will be fine."

When I snort, and say, "I don't think you can teach me anything my mom hasn't already grilled me about, anyway," Betsy lets out a short laugh and reaches over to pat my hand. "I'm sure you're quite right, Meg."

Afterward, I help Betsy with the dishes (good practice for my B&B work), then Carl escorts me down the path to the cottage. I'm glad of his industrial-strength flashlight, as the new moon has a hard time penetrating the dense darkness of the island night. No streetlights or headlights; no light pollution here.

We follow the beam to the bottom of the steep wooden steps leading to the cottage veranda and that, I think, is when the penny drops for both of us. When we stop walking, and our feet stop crunch-crunching on the gravel, and we're surrounded by the quiet of the country night, is when it suddenly dawns on us that I'm staying in this windblown cottage, perched on the edge of the bay, surrounded by acres and acres of fields, by myself.

Not the end of the world, but a little isolating, and feeling even more so now as Carl and I stand in the small circle of light pushing back the dark.

The easy, chatty conversation we've been having about the weather, and Carl's new sailboat, stops abruptly and "So ..." says Carl and "Well ..." I answer, then add quickly "I'd better go in."

"Are you ..." Carl starts, but switches gears to ask, "Do you have everything you need?" and I say "Yes," and "Thank you again for dinner," and "See you tomorrow morning!" and hurry into the cottage holding a smile on my face, shooting the deadbolt behind me.

I want to follow him and yell, "Stay! Please stay!" or "Let me go back with you!" but this is Night One of weeks and months of nights to come. I just need to get used to it. Used to the profound blackness all around. Used to the ceaseless moaning of the wind around the eaves, and the occasional gust against the window panes. Used to all the sounds the little wooden cottage makes that are different from the ones made by our big old brick house in Ottawa.

I brush my teeth in record time, skip washing my face, and jump into the bed, pulling the covers up and over my ears.

I've left the curtains open a crack, so I can just glimpse Carl and Betsy's house all lit up across the fields. *It's right there. Not too far. Just a quick sprint.* I scrunch my eyes shut, close my hand around Major's braid, tucked under my pillow, force my breathing into an even rhythm, and am asleep before the B&B lights go out.

****

I sit bolt upright, gasp for air, then hold my breath to listen. *There was a sound.* But all I hear is the humming of the ceiling fan; the sawing of the crickets floating through the screen.

I blink. The shadows are in the wrong places, and the door isn't where it should be. I'm dizzy with disorientation.

My heart flutters under my ribcage, and there's a slick of sweat on my forearms and, when I reach to rub it, at the back of my neck.

Where am I? My eyes find the crack in the curtains, revealing the moon long and low over the fields outside. *The cottage.*

My breathing evens, pulse slows. *It's OK.* I'm OK. I'm in the big loft bedroom at the cottage. I'm all alone. There's nobody here.

Why is the fan on high? With the covers off, goose bumps rise in my arms.

Why did I come here?

What have I done?

As soon as the panic recedes, emptiness takes its place. No tears; just an expanding ache in my chest. I miss Major, Slate, Chester. I miss my dad and my persnickety mom and even Craig; who I have never before thought about in the middle of the night.

Snap out of it. This was my choice. And, anyway, being back in Ottawa wouldn't solve anything.

I shake my head. "Suck it up, buttercup." It's strange to be able to talk out loud in the middle of the night, without worrying about waking anyone else up.

Maybe some warm milk. The worn stair treads are soft under my feet.

In the kitchen the hum and beep of the microwave are familiar, friendly. Microwaves everywhere follow the same soundtrack.

I curl my fingers around the warm mug, and a memory jumps into my head. My mom, in a robe, lit only by the under cabinet glow in our kitchen, warming milk for me. "This should make you sleepy. It always works for me."

We didn't always fight.

I pad out to the living room, my bare feet scuff-scuffing on the wood floors.

I curl up on the sofa facing the picture window, and sip my drink, and let the ever-shifting water of the moon-bathed river mesmerize me.

It's hypnotic, and I'm nodding off when a ship skims into view.

Slipping, gliding, motoring through the night. It would be near-invisible – just an inkier patch of dark in the pitch of the night – were it not for the strings of lights outlining the bow and stern; pinpricking the space in between with flickering dots of incandescence.

A fairy ship.

With it comes the noise; a rhythmic thrum. Something I can feel, as well as hear. The working of the huge ship's engines reverberating through all the layers of water, and rock, and earth, and man-built foundation, and floor between it and me.

Turbines turning, pistons pumping, doing whatever all the parts of an engine that massive do. One thing's for sure; they aren't quiet.

This is different. This is magical. This is me, not in Kansas anymore.

The thought takes me back to bed, and into sleep, until I'm wakened by light seeping in around the edges of the curtains, and the realization that I need to get up soon and go to work.

Chapter Six

Showered, dressed, wide awake, I walk into chaos Carl and Betsy style. Chaos with a smile, and a calm tone of voice, and an assurance everything will be OK.

What should be a quiet morning, with just one room occupied overnight, has been turned upside-down by one of the guests – the husband – sauntering casually into the kitchen to ask what time he and his wife should leave to catch the ferry for their nine-thirty appointment in Kingston.

Carl looks at Betsy, and Betsy looks at Carl, and they both look at the clock with "five minutes ago" written all over their faces. The nine o'clock weekday ferry is one of the busiest ones leaving the island, and it's nearly eight now.

While I'm thinking *no way, too bad, so sad,* Carl and Betsy switch smoothly into high gear.

Carl is smiling and pleasant. "Well, the thing to do if you want to make that ferry is to give me your keys. I'll take your car in now, and put it in line, and Meg can drive you into the village when you're ready."

The man frowns. "Really? Is that necessary?"

Betsy nods. "Yes, you see, that's one of the main commuter ferries. Lots of the Islanders who work in Kingston will be trying to get on it, and there will already be a line-up. Carl needs to go soon to make sure your car gets on."

I tackle the dishes already piling up by the sink from Betsy's early morning breakfast-making activities, and observe while Carl takes the keys, and Betsy sends the man back upstairs with strict instructions for him and his wife to be ready to go in half an hour.

When it's just Betsy and me again, I point to a picture frame hanging on the kitchen wall. It contains a list headed "Words to Live by" with sayings underneath like, "It might never happen" and "A problem shared is a problem halved" and "Perfect is the enemy of good. "

"You're missing one." I scrub at a Pyrex dish, trying to scrape free a stubborn bit of baked-on coffee cake. "How does it go? 'Lack of planning on your part does not constitute an emergency on our part?' Isn't that it?"

"I know what you mean." She's setting up the coffee maker to have a fresh pot ready when the tardy travelers descend. "But, I'm afraid, when you run a B&B it actually does."

"People – even people who are normally very organized – tend to switch off their brains when they're on holidays."

"They come to an island to get away – to forget about everything – they don't think of schedules, or ferries, or real life, until the last minute, which can sometimes be too late.

She winks, and smiles. "Then it's up to us to try to make it right for them."

OK. I thought my first lesson would be how to make a bed. Or a tutorial on using the washing machine. Instead, I've been subtly asked to re-arrange my thinking on customer service.

"In other words, the customer's always right?"

Betsy laughs. "You got it. Except when they're not; which only happens on very rare occasions." The phone rings, and she reaches for it. "Yes? Great. Thanks for doing that. See you soon."

She hangs up and turns to me. "Carl's got their car in line, and he says they'll make it with about five spots to spare." She looks at the clock. "As soon as they come down you'd better leave; I'll pack up their breakfast to go."

Then, as an afterthought, adds, "That's fine right? You don't mind driving them, do you? Because I can go …"

I interrupt. "No, it'll be fine." I'm still not supposed to drive without a licensed driver in the car, but clearly at least one of the guests is licensed, and Carl will drive back with me, so it's all good. "It's my pleasure."

She nods, smiles. "You'll do just fine here, Meg."

It's a nice way to start my career at the B&B. Skimming along the tire-smoothed, faded-out asphalt on a beautiful day; sunny with big, blue skies, floating white clouds, a soft breeze nodding and swaying the crops and pastures we speed by. Lovely, lovely, lovely; a picture postcard of summer.

The McLellans – the tardy guests – chat to one another, pointing out new calves frolicking next to their mothers, red-tailed hawks swooping hopefully over fields.

I slow as we pass a girl riding a sturdy buckskin horse, and she raises her hand in a half wave.

"So nice to see, isn't it?" Mrs. McLellan asks. "I've always wanted to learn to ride but it's just one of those things I've never gotten around to."

I ride. In fact I show. In fact I had my own horse. Until he died... I bite my tongue, nod, and make a "hmmm" noise, and keep driving.

Just because I'm sad, doesn't mean it's OK to dump my grief on innocent guests, who've paid for a getaway.

In fact, I'm sure that would be on Betsy's list of words to live by: "Listening to your problems is not part of a guest's ideal B&B experience."

See? This job is good for me. Focusing on other people leaves less room for grief.

The McLellans are charmed when we slow down to pass a tractor, and the farmer tips his hat. I sketch him a wave.

"Do you know him?" Mrs. McLellan asks.

"Oh, no ma'am. That's just the way it's done on the island. It's rude not to wave."

"Too bad. He was a nice-looking young man; not much older than you, I wouldn't have thought."

I smile. She reminds me of my grandmother with her "nice-looking young man." It's a generational thing, I guess, talking that way. What I don't know is whether it's something that'll die with her generation, or whether someday I'll start talking that way too. Wearing "slacks" instead of pants, and replacing "hot" with "handsome" or "nice-looking."

As we enter the village, we cruise down a long line of cars before reaching Carl, and the McLellans' safely parked car.

I find their eyes in the rear-view mirror. "None of these people we're passing will make it onto the nine o'clock boat."

Their eyebrows rise. "We never thought of it being busy."

"Well, not to worry. Carl's got you sorted out."

I pull up beside their car, and pop the trunk so Carl can transfer their luggage from his car to theirs.

"Go find a place to park," Carl tells me. "I'll meet you at the bakery."

I open my mouth to explain I can't – not on my own – then shut it again. *Things are different here.*

This is the island. Police have to come over on the ferry with all the other cars. They drive off the ramp, and down the main street, in full view of everyone in the village. Most island kids drive farm machinery before they hit double digits; I don't think a sixteen-year-old with her G2 license driving three blocks to the closest parking spot is going to make any waves.

So I break the rule, and I don't get caught. I ease Carl's car into a wide-open spot alongside a row of white-painted rocks on somebody's front lawn, then walk the few short steps to the bakery with a spring in my step and a smile stretching my cheeks.

A beautiful morning, a successful solo drive, and now the bakery. Cinnamon, chocolate, lemon and yeast; my mouth waters at the combination of these smells together. I sit on the rickety wooden bench outside the front door and breathe in the warm, sweet scents, and watch the world go by.

Coming here was so the right thing to do.

"Morning." I raise my eyes. Mrs. McLellan's nice-looking young man is tipping his hat to me for the second time today.

"Where's your tractor?" *Meg. You. Are. An. Idiot.* Could I think of a stupider thing to say? Slate would nail me for that one.

This guy's not Slate, though. A deep, slow smile starts in one corner of his mouth, and travels all the way to the other corner, lighting up the rest of his face as it goes.

"Funny girl." He gives me an extra little nod before shouldering his way through the door and into the delicious smells of the bakery.

And, while I don't know exactly what he means, or if it's good or bad, I do suddenly see that he *is* a very nice-looking young man.

Chapter Seven

Another night, another heart-racing, sweaty, midnight awakening.

I lift my hand to wipe my sticky forehead, and the small braid I didn't even realize I was holding, falls into my lap.

I stare at it for a minute. Why have I even kept this? What it really shows is how desperately I was trying to save myself as my horse went down under me. Gripping so hard, I ripped a chunk of his mane out, while he fell and died with strangers around him.

I should have gone to him. Should have gotten up and pushed my way through; crawled if I had to.

But I didn't.

Slate said it, Craig said it, the vet said it; he was dead before he hit the ground. He didn't feel anything. He probably died happy – lifting for a jump – the thing he loved most.

Sometimes the thought comforts me; just not in the middle of the night.

Not now.

I pull the noisy chain on the bedside lamp. Fumble for my paperback splayed on the floor. Read until my eyes droop shut.

"Are you OK, Meg? You look tired."

I press my fingers to the thin skin under my eyes where I noticed dark, bruise-like smudges in the mirror this morning. "I'm fine," I tell Betsy. "Stayed up too late reading."

Not exactly a lie.

"I hope so. It's going to be a busy day."

"Yes. Fine. Absolutely. I can do it."

By six o'clock, three of my fingernails are broken into jagged stubs, and my left arm aches from wrist to shoulder, but every window in the house is clean. The back of my neck is sunburned a roasting pink, but the vegetable garden is free of weeds. My eyes are red, and still sting a bit, but the onions and green peppers are chopped for tomorrow's omelette breakfast.

By the time I get back to the cottage, I'm too tired to make anything resembling a real dinner. Two pieces of toast. A sliced apple. A tin of cream of tomato soup that's been in the cupboard for I-don't-know-how-long. It means I finish the dishes quickly, then stand at the kitchen sink, hands immersed in sudsy water, zoned out as I watch the last rays of the setting sun pick out the peaks of the ripples in the bay.

Which is when it comes. A howl; long and mournful, carried clear across the fields and meadows of the island. But how many fields? I try to picture the coyote that set up this howl. Is he alone or with a pack?

Yip-yip-aroooooo...Yip-yip-arooooooo... The howls come again, this time in varying registers, overlapping one-another.

A pack, then. Out there, somewhere, celebrating a kill, or marking their territory, or maybe just saluting the rising moon.

Also out there is my bike, abandoned in the gravel after I used it to ride up the driveway to secure the gate, which was swinging in the ever-strengthening wind.

I sigh and step out into the intensifying dusk, and a gust of building wind. It's a struggle to wrestle my bike into the shed past a precarious pile of boogie boards and a three-person inflatable hot dog. While I'm inside, the door blows shut behind me and I stand, frozen, in the dark while another round of howls whips up.

Is it my imagination, or are they closer?

As I'm walking back across the yard, a solitary howl drifts in from the east; soft at first then building, gathering, swelling in volume and intensity.

It's so beautiful it feels wrong to walk, move, do anything else but just listen to it – soak it in – but the hairs on my arms, standing on end, and the adrenaline quickening my breathing, urge me otherwise.

Go. Move. Now.

I scoot inside the cottage and lock the door behind me.

Time to face the new reality of my evenings, which are solitary and very quiet. After that last howl even the coyotes have given up.

We have a TV, but the channel selection is rock bottom. I can watch *The Bachelor*, *Gone Fishin'*, *The Bachelor*, a re-run of the Winnipeg Just for Laughs Comedy Festival or *The Bachelor*. I do a final run up, then down the channels and find one more station offering a blurry, interference-laced episode of – yup – *The Bachelor.*

I have a laptop, but no internet connection, and the service on my cheap cell phone is spotty at best.

I could call Slate, but what would I say? 'I've learned how to clean windows without leaving streaks?' or 'Just this morning I collected the eggs for tomorrow's omelettes straight from Betsy's chickens?'

I can just hear her: 'You know how to party Megsters!'

Instead I thumb out a text: Have already been driving (and already cleaning). Already met a guy, too – don't get excited – not what you think: cowboy. Talk later.

I press "send" and leave the phone positioned on the coat hook/shelf in the front hall, where it seems to get the best reception. The message will go eventually.

I hesitate, then pick the phone up again, scroll to the message my mom sent yesterday, asking how the first day of work went. Reply: Work is good. Cottage is clean. I am fine. How is Chester? Oh, and Dad, too. Bye for now.

With the social part of my evening behind me, I grab a Diet Coke, and a bag of Doritos, and tromp up the stairs to bed, to the book I half-finished at two o'clock this morning.

As I settle into my bed to read, I mentally edit my text to my mom: Eating chips in bed. Delicious! Crumbs everywhere.

Another howl rises through the now-dark air outside, and my smile disappears. I need a good sleep tonight and those howls aren't the lullaby I'm looking for.

"Don't!" My voice bounces back to me under the low eaves of the long room. I shake my head. *It's over.* There's no way to change what happened to Major. Why can't my night-time brain accept what my daytime mind knows?

I go back to the beginning of the page, to re-read all the words I didn't take in the first time. I'm fine. This is good. I'll let the story distract me.

Which would be a great plan, if it wasn't for the tear drop staining the paper before I even get to the bottom of the page.

Chapter Eight

There's no sleeping late, here. While the fields surrounding the cottage never stop humming with noise, at dawn the buzz intensifies from soft cricket songs, and gentle owl hoots, to the trills of tree swallows and bobolinks. *Wake up! Wake up! Wake up!*

Even the waves seem to lap at the shore a little more loudly and, as soon as it nudges above the horizon, the rising sun spotlights my east-facing window.

I yank my hair into a pony tail and swap my sleep shirt for a t-shirt and running shorts. When I step through the screen door, the boards of the porch are soft and already sun-warmed under my sock feet. I toe my running shoes on, and skip every second step on my way down to the gravel driveway.

It's a gorgeous time to run. It's been a hot spring, and the summer's stoking up to be no different. By mid-morning, the air pulses with heat.

Not at six a.m. though.

It's fresh. In places it's even chilly. In the dips of the road, where the fog lies thick and wet, the temperature drops, raising goose bumps on my skin. Things are visible this early in the morning that get blocked out later, as the hot sun rises.

Spider webs glimmer everywhere, beautiful on barbed-wire fences, shimmering between stalks of hay, their steely strands picked out by sunlit dew.

I run hard and fast, trying to drive away the fatigue building from my interrupted nights. Seeking energy to get me through my work days which are tiring both physically (carrying suitcases, making beds, vacuuming endlessly) and mentally (smiling all day long, answering the same questions over and over again, saying "of course I'll bring you tea," when I know they ordered coffee).

Most mornings I flush wild turkeys out of the long grass by the side of the road. Often I see the deer, sometimes with her fawn, sometimes not. "Where's your baby?" I call, and her thin-skinned ears cup in my direction, honing in on my signal like translucent satellite dishes.

Every morning, the same dog barks at me. He's a big German Shepherd but his wagging tail tells me he barks from compulsion, not malice; barks because he can't not bark. Barks, a little bit, because he'd like to be coming with me, following me up the gravel rise to where the Old Concession Line crosses Split Oak Road, to where the cows congregate waiting to be let through the gate for their morning feed.

He can't follow me though, because he clearly has an important job where he is. There's a big old farmhouse to guard and, presumably, a family inside, so no gallivanting for Rex, as I've come to think of him. On the second day, I started bringing him dog treats.

At first, he wouldn't take the treat from me. He barked and barked and barked, and I imagined him saying, 'Look at me. I'm doing my job. I'm not being distracted by dog biscuits and running.' I left the treat lying in the grass beside the driveway, and he glanced at it between barks.

When I passed the house on the way back, Rex was nowhere in sight and the dog biscuit was gone.

The next day he picked it off the ground while I watched him.

Today he takes it from me, but makes sure to bark before and after, just to make it clear he's doing his job.

Rex makes me miss Chester. Maybe that would be all I need – a big, friendly dog – to curl up with me and soothe me through the night.

Slate's texts always make me smile, and I want it to stay that way. Don't want to turn our light, fun, back-and-forth into a pity party, so I tell her the good, and the funny, and keep quiet about the tough things.

I've even come to count on my mom's messages reminding me to wipe down the microwave after I use it, and to clear leftovers out of the fridge at the end of the week.

The thing about texts, though, is I almost feel more alone after I've read them. Like the person was with me for a few, brief seconds, and now they're gone.

Sometimes I think it would be nice to have a more constant companion. I don't think I could convince Rex to come home with me, though.

Put-put-put. What *is* that noise?

The low-slanting sun waters my eyes as I squint over my shoulder.

It's a tractor, going very slowly. There's a guy in a baseball cap behind the big wheel. I wave, as is the island way, and move far over to the rough verge of the road, giving him a clear path to pass me.

He pulls up beside me, and I nod in his direction without really looking. I keep running and wait to be able to reclaim the smoother centre of the road.

No such luck; he's still there. I keep moving, look straight ahead, trying to hold onto my running rhythm despite the rattle of the tractor engine beside me. *Put your foot down.*

Nothing happens; he's still there. A sideways glance tells me he's fit – or, at least, he doesn't have the beer belly prevalent on so many of the older farmers around here. Then he turns a smiling face to me, and I recognize the guy from the highway, the guy from the bakery: "Where's your tractor?" guy.

Maybe my blush won't be noticeable in my already running-flushed cheeks.

He's yelling, but I can't hear a word over the rumbling of the tractor. I shrug, shake my head and keep running.

The tractor starts to slow. It eases off a bit, then some more and, within a few metres, idles to a halt.

Without noticing – without intending to – I also come to a stop. Or at least a jog on the spot. So much for my rhythm.

"Hi," says the guy from his perch way up on the tractor seat.

"Hi."

"Jared," he says, and I say "Meg."

"Are you the one who's been waking up my dog every morning?" He's smiling, so I don't think he's serious, but it's hard to know for sure.

"Well, as far as I can tell your dog's already awake when I come by."

"Good point. Rex."

"Pardon me?"

"His name's Rex." In the shade under the brim of his cap, his eyes narrow. "Are you OK? You look strange."

I've stopped moving. Am just standing, stock-still. *His name's Rex* ... I shake my head. "Uh, I'm fine, thanks."

"He's friendly."

"I know, I like him. Is it OK if he runs with me?"

"Fine. Just whistle and he should go."

"Alright." And then, the same geeky part of me that started the whole tractor thing in the first place surfaces again. "I see you found your tractor."

Instant change. In him. In the atmosphere between us. Sparks, chemistry or something, ignited by my stupid joke, fanned by that same molasses-smooth-and-slow smile from the other day.

"Still funny," he says.

Something twangs deep in my gut. A twist, a lurch, a feeling like nervousness, but edged with pleasure. "I don't know about that. I'm not exactly known for my wit."

"Hmmm," he does something to the tractor – something involving gears, I suspect – and the engine gets louder again. "We'll see."

"We'll see?"

"We'll see!" And he's off, lumbering away, with one last wave for me.

I sprint a few strides, my eyes on his straight, strong back, then slip back into a steadier pace; one I can sustain all the way home.

And as I run, two words cycle through my head. *We'll see-we'll see-we'll see.*

Back at the cottage my charging phone holds a text:

Slate: Bronc-riding cowboy, or tractor-driving cowboy?

My reply: Oh, he definitely drives a tractor.

My cell reception's good this morning, because Slate's reply pops up before I leave for work: YAIT. Tractor = boring. Keep looking Miss Meg.

Slate doesn't care if acronyms mean anything to anyone else, as long as they work for her. I spend my whole walk to the B&B working on her latest one. *YAIT. Y.A.I.T.* What the ... It pops into my head as I step onto Carl's mowed lawn. Oh! "Yawning as I type."

I smile. Funny, because the last thing Jared makes me want to do is yawn.

Chapter Nine

I t's a beautiful summer evening and I'm in the village, on a mission to replenish my reading-in-bed snack supply.

I shouldn't be here this late, but this afternoon one of the B&B guests started having chest pains. "I'll be fine," he insisted when I found him sitting on a mostly decorative chair in the hallway, clutching his left arm. "I just need some water."

Not only did I get the water, I got Betsy too. "He's kind of grey," I told her.

It took her one look, and two seconds to decide. "I'm driving him to the ferry. Call 911 and tell them we're on our way."

With Betsy gone, and Carl cutting brush at the edge of the far field, I was alone in a house which was very much not ready for an onslaught of breakfast guests in the morning. I did the best I could to mix ingredients for muffins, then made a salad out of random pieces of fruit left in the fridge and fruit bowl. Tidied up the kitchen and, meeting Carl on my way out, explained what had happened.

Stumbled down the path to the cottage tired, hungry and looking forward to a relaxing evening, which is when I discovered no Diet Coke, and no Doritos.

Checked my watch, and decided I could just make it to the village and back before sunset *if* I started immediately, and *if* I pedaled hard. Both of which I did, and made it to the general store in decent time.

I'm zipping my panniers closed on a twelve-pack of DC, two pounds of new potatoes, a carton of orange juice, and a family-sized bag of Doritos, when I notice a problem. A fairly major problem. "Shit!"

I look around, ready to apologize for my language, but there's nobody in sight. "Shit," I mutter again. I have a flat tire. Very flat. When I push down on my handlebars, the rubber pancakes on the pavement.

This is a working island, a rural island; a place where nails, and barbed wire, and other sharp and piercing things are a fact of life. Flat tires aren't surprising but, like this one, they're never particularly convenient.

With a click and a hum, the light outside the general store powers to life. It's getting dark.

God, I am so stupid. I shouldn't have come. Should have made do with well water and saltines.

I trap my lip between my teeth and gaze past all the empty parking spots in front of the closed post office, bakery and coffee shop. There isn't even the shortest of ferry lines – the boat pulled out five minutes ago, and people aren't exactly queuing up to get off the island at this time on a weekday evening.

No. They're safe at home, watching TV, getting ready for bed.
Like I should be.

I don't want to go back into the store. Don't want to ask to
borrow the phone. Don't want to disturb Carl and Betsy – not that I
even know if Betsy is back from dealing with the hospital-bound
guest – and have to say "I'm stupid" and "I'm stuck" and "Would
someone please, please come and get me?"

In the quiet evening, voices grab my attention. Two figures
walking up from the ferry dock – one in the high visibility vests
worn by the ferry crew – the other wearing a familiar uniform of
jeans, t-shirt, baseball cap.

It could be anyone …

But it's not. He takes a package from the ferry guy, and the
voice that says, "Thanks, again, for picking this up, Doug," is
Jared's. I'd already know it anywhere.

My stomach knots. *Jared.*

A car crawling down the street rolls to a stop, and the ferry
worker gets in. "'Night Jared."

"'Night." Jared lifts his hand in a half-wave, and turns away
from me.

Shit. There goes my drive home.

Ask him.

I can't.

Why not? Ask him.

'Oh for God's sake, Meg; if you don't ask him I will!' – I'm
channeling Slate when I take a deep breath, and ask, "Jared?"

He half-turns, shrugs, and keeps walking.

I step into the pool of light shed by the sign. "Jared! Jared!"

He stops this time, turns around completely, and walks back toward me with a smile spreading, slow and friendly, across his face.

"Nice night for a bike ride."

"Would be if my bike wasn't broken." I point to the tire. Now I'm smiling too. It's amazing how fast relief can push despair out of the way.

Jared bends down, tests the tire, straightens up and pushes his baseball cap back. "Well, unfortunately I don't seem to have my tractor with me tonight ..."

I give a half nod – a *you-got-me* nod.

"... but I think I can remember where I left my pick-up, if you wouldn't mind me giving you a lift back in that."

"I think I could settle for a pick-up," I say.

****

It's accomplished in no time. Bike – complete with flat tire – in the back of the pick-up, me installed in the high cab, loving the space of the long bench seat, the sparseness of the dashboard, the absence of any clutter.

"You like it?" There's laughter in Jared's voice as he catches me caressing the ridged vinyl of the seat on either side of me. "It's real Corinthian leather, you know."

He says it like I know what he means; like it's an inside reference we already share. His tone invites me to enter the joke with him, so I do. I smile, then laugh, and let the laugh be mostly at myself. It feels good.

"I love old pick-up trucks," I say.

"You spend a lot of time in them?"

"I ride." I hesitate, backpedal. "*Rode.* I rode. A lot. For most of my life."

He looks at me for a long minute with questions in his eyes. *Please don't ask.*

The best defence is a good offense, and talking is my only weapon.

I tap the window behind my head. "So, I hear they might close. Does that affect you?"

"What?"

"The agricultural college. How far into the program are you?" *Please don't say "I've graduated" – that would mean too many years between us ...* I pinch the inside of my wrist ... *Now I'm being an idiot. Too many years for what?*

He turns to me, his brow furrowed. "How did you ..."

"The sticker. From the college. On your back window. I saw it when you loaded my bike in."

"Oh. That. No."

"No, what?"

"No, it doesn't affect me."

"Oh. Why? Are you done?"

"You could say that."

His half-answers are making me twitch. "What, exactly, does..."

He holds up his hand and brakes at the same time. "Sshhh. Listen."

The coyotes again. Baying, howling, saluting the moon. The notes float and twist and rise in a spiral to the starry sky.

"Nice."

His easy smile comes back. "Isn't it? As long as they stay far away from the cattle."

The truck picks up speed again. The long, straight highway is smooth, and warm evening air breezes through the open windows. I stretch my legs into the deep footwell and lean back. "So, cattle?"

He nods. "Beef. And hay. And some soy."

YAIT. I shake my head. *Get out of my head, Slate.*

"Hard work," I say.

He shrugs. "I try to stay on top of things, which is basically impossible."

"Hence the tractor driving?"

"Yup. Couldn't do half of what I do without the tractor. Speaking of which ..." We turn off the highway and his headlights sweep across shiny metal, massive tires with v-shaped treads.

"New?"

"Used, but new to me. I try to take care of it."

We coast to a stop in the gravel by the tractor, and Jared cuts the engine. Rex whines at the side of the truck, tail sweeping, waiting to greet me, and there's a woman stepping out the side door. She's drying her hands on a tea towel, with flour dusting one cheek.

Wow, I can't believe how pretty she is. Or maybe attractive is a better word – it's one my mom uses all the time – one that, to me, sounds stilted and old-fashioned but, with this woman, it fits. There's something undeniably *attractive* about her.

She's clearly Jared's mom. I know it even before he says "Hey, Mom." I know from the coarse, sandy not-quite-curly-but-more-than-wavy hair they share. From the tight stretch of skin over high cheekbones. From the intriguing crinkles at the corner of their eyes that speak of sun, and smiles, and wide-open spaces.

"Hi there! I'm Jane Strickland." Jared's mom says this, not quite as though we've known each other forever, but as though this could be the first step in us getting there. Instead of holding out her hand, she squeezes my shoulders in a sort of mini-hug.

"Pie ready?" Jared asks.

"Cherry," she confirms, and saliva springs into my mouth. I love cherry pie, and I have a feeling she makes a good one.

"Can you join us for pie, Meg?" My mouth is open to ask how she knows my name, when she says "Nothing's a secret on this island, Meg, you must know that. Betsy and I are good friends."

I follow her into a kitchen that would have my mom calling in renovators on the spot but, to me, looks country perfect down to the last, old-fashioned linoleum tile.

The cherry pie is amazing. Delicious, mouth-watering, and nicely tangy, while staying just the right side of too-sweet.

"I love this pie!" I clap my hand over my mouth, realizing I may not be one hundred per cent done chewing.

"Yeah, my mom knows which grocery store makes the best pie."

Jared ducks as she throws her napkin at him. "As Jared well knows, I started baking as soon as I got home from work yesterday, so he could have pie for his birthday, which means I got to bed late. He should be careful, because I'm grumpy when I'm sleep deprived."

"It's your ... oh, I am so sorry ... I shouldn't be here ... I ..." I give up, drop my fork, hide my red cheeks behind my hands.

"Don't be silly!" Jared's mom says. "Having you here is a treat. Another piece, either of you?"

Jared nods a yes, and while she lifts the knife to cut another slice, she smoothes over my awkwardness with a question. "So, what brings you here this summer, Meg?"

"Oh. I usually show all summer – horse shows; I horseback ride – but I ..." I hesitate, but something about Jared saving me, and his mom welcoming me, makes me want to tell them. "... I lost my horse at the beginning of the season."

She hands Jared his pie, but keeps her attention on me. "That sounds difficult."

I nod. "It was. He died right on the course. I was thrown and I couldn't get to him. I had a concussion. I didn't get to say good-bye." My voice is thickening now. "Oh, gosh, I'm sorry. I didn't mean to say all that. I need to learn when to shut up."

Jared's shaking head catches my eye, and I turn to him.

"Don't do that," he says.

"Don't do what?"

"Don't shut up. If you were a quiet person, I wouldn't have driven you home tonight and then I'd be stuck alone with my mom on my birthday."

"Jared Strickland!" His mom reaches over and pulls his remaining pie away from him. "I think you've just insulted both of us at once!"

"It's OK Mrs. Strickland. I'm not insulted. If *he* was a quiet person, I'd still be telling my sad story, and we'd all be crying by now."

Jared holds both palms up. "See? Can I have my pie back now?"

"Apologize to Meg."

"I'm sorry Meg."

She slides Jared's plate back in front of him, then indicates a sliver of pie with her knife, and points to my plate, "So? Pie?"

I blink, take a deep breath, and smile. "Yes, please. I can't resist."

I take a bite. I've never had pie this good before. My text to Slate will go something like this – Tractor-driving cowboy's mother bakes out-of-this-world cherry pie: less boring?

****

Jared's mom is arranging dishes in the dishwasher while I clear the table.

"You don't have to do that," she says.

"It's a side-effect of working for Betsy. I can't sit still in the kitchen."

The screen door opens on Jared, backlit, standing in the doorway. "I'm ready to go if you are, Meg."

"Sure, I'll be right there."

I rinse my hands, and dry them on the towel Jared's mother hands me. "Thank you so much for inviting me in. It was really nice."

This time she gives me a full-on hug. "I meant it when I said it was a treat to have you. Please make sure you come around again. I sometimes think Jared's life is too serious. He needs to have more fun."

As I'm stepping out across the yard to where Jared waits by the truck, she calls after me. "If you come again, I'll make more pie!"

Jared drives me home, with Rex perched half on the pick-up seat, half on my lap. They walk to the front door with me, a set of work boots clump-clumping on the porch boards alongside the click-clack of Rex's nails.

"Thanks," I say to Jared, and then have no idea what to say or do next. I've never stood on my doorstep with a guy before – other than Carl, who's a grandpa, not a *guy*. So I bend down to hug Rex, bury my face in his furry neck. I stroke his ears, then stand up. "Thanks again."

"My pleasure."

I'm still thinking of how nice that sounds – *my pleasure* – as I watch his taillights retreat: disappearing, then popping back up, as the wind sways the tall grasses back and forth across the driveway.

My pleasure. I creak upstairs to the bedroom – *my pleasure* – and fall asleep picturing Jared in his wear-softened jeans and once-white t-shirt, with his sun-browned face and windmessed hair.

Chapter Ten

Every day before I push through the screen door into the kitchen, with its morning smells of baking and coffee, I walk around the house to the chicken coop snugged in the shady side yard beside the much-larger garage.

I unlatch the sturdy wooden door with the reinforcing boards exed across it, and make the half-step up onto the hollow-sounding plywood floor.

Inside, the breeze blows through the rusty screens on the big side windows, and dust motes float in the rays of light pushing through the chinks in the old boards.

The hens live in an oasis of serenity. They want for nothing, need nothing they aren't given. Eat when they feel like it, drink when they want to, and lay big, perfect, chalky-shelled eggs in abundance.

When I step out of the coop with four fresh eggs in my collecting basket and one cupped carefully in my hand, its residual heat sinking into my palm, a familiar-looking pick-up truck is disappearing down the driveway, a cloud of dust ribboning behind it as it turns onto the gravel road.

Jared? "Jared!" My bike, not just with two firm round tires, but also shiny clean, is propped up against the split rail fence by Betsy's vegetable garden.

When I carry the eggs back into the kitchen, Betsy gives me a one-eyebrow-up-one-eyebrow-down look. "I heard you yell ..."

"My bike. I had a flat tire in the village last night. Jared drove me home – you know, Jared Strickland – he fixed my bike and he just dropped it off. It's like new."

Betsy nods. "Well, you could do worse than to be rescued by Jared Strickland."

Do not blush, do not blush ... "His mom was really nice, too. She invited me in for pie. It was delicious. I wish I could thank them."

"I could help with that."

"Oh yeah?"

"I was going to make lemon loaf today anyway; why don't we just double the recipe and you can take one up to the Stricklands?" She reaches for the egg basket. "We've definitely got enough eggs."

Betsy lies her recipe book flat on the counter – more for my benefit than hers – she must know all these recipes by heart. I follow the ingredients list; rummaging flour, sugar and salt from the cupboards. She hands me a lemon. "Here, do you want to zest this while I get started on the mixing?"

I scrape the dimpled yellow lemon rind against the grater, and the sharp smell hits my nostrils. I wrinkle my nose. "I love lemon."

"So does Jared. A long time ago, for one of the church suppers, I made a couple of lemon meringue pies. I was helping serve them up, and we ran out of the first one. When I went to look for the second one, it was nowhere in sight. I was going crazy wondering where that second pie had gone when Jared's dad brought him up to me. He couldn't have been more than five at the time, and he had lemon on his chin, and meringue on his nose."

"Cute."

"Very."

I look up and catch Betsy's eyes. *Don't blush. Move on.* "His dad wasn't there last night."

She sighs. Shakes her head. "No. Rob died."

I gasp. "He what?" Plenty of my friends' parents have divorced. None have died. A pang of guilt runs through me for not returning the phone message my mom left yesterday. *I'll definitely call today.*

Betsy's nodding. "It was last fall – just after Thanksgiving. Rob was clearing a stump in one of the back fields. He always worked so hard – he had another job as well as working on the farm – and I guess he was tired; maybe in a hurry. He didn't attach the chain the way he should have, and his tractor flipped over."

"His *tractor*?" By far my most frequent topic of conversation with Jared so far. *Where's your tractor?* "He must hate me."

"What?"

"Nothing. It's just, I had no idea. I've probably said some stupid things."

Betsy props her wooden spoon against the mixing bowl, where it drips into the batter. She reaches for my bowl of lemon zest. "Meg, please don't worry. Nobody could expect you to know." She dumps the zest into the bowl. "It's been hard on Jared – there's no doubt he's had some issues – so I'm sure he's just relieved to have somebody new to talk to, somebody who doesn't know all his business."

Knowing what Jared's been through makes me feel stupid, sheltered, spoiled. Oh God, I sat there and told him – and his mom – about Major dying. How ridiculous must I have sounded, to be mourning a *horse*.

I stick a stray curl of lemon zest on the end of my tongue, just to feel the bitter taste.

"You OK?" Betsy asks.

"Uh-huh, fine. Just ... you know."

She nods. "I know."

When the timer goes off, I run in from the clothesline to find Betsy's beaten me to it, and is lifting the lemon loaf out of the oven. It's springy and yellow, with a jagged split down the middle just waiting for the drizzle of Betsy's magic lemon syrup.

In sharp contrast to the heavenly baking is the state of the rest of the kitchen. I put my hands on my hips and take in the toaster surrounded by crumbs, the grill shining with bacon fat, the mini-compost bin overflowing with peels, and cores, and seeds, and the stacks and stacks of congealing breakfast dishes.

Betsy catches my eye. "I know. Looks like a bomb went off, doesn't it?"

"And the guests are all checking out, aren't they?" Meaning no light cleaning; all the beds to be stripped and re-made, bathrooms to be scrubbed top to bottom and laundry, laundry, laundry.

"Yes, they are. But we can do it. In fact, I'm so sure we can do it that I'll make you a deal. I'll start here, you start upstairs, and when we're done, that's it; you're finished for the day."

"But won't you need help prepping for tomorrow, or weeding the garden?"

Betsy shakes her head. "You have two priorities today: put those rooms right and deliver this lemon loaf while it's still fresh."

"I'm not sure. Maybe, I …"

Betsy puts her hands on her hips, pulls herself up tall so she's eye-to-eye with me. "Meg Traherne."

"Yes?"

"Is this about you?"

I think of being rescued from the village. Cherry pie. My shiny bike waiting for me outside. "No."

"So, go!"

I go.

****

It sounds good; getting off work early on a beautiful afternoon to deliver fresh lemon loaf. A bike ride in the country. How nice. How relaxing. *How bloody hard can this be?*

I'm used to running this route, and you can drive it in a zip, but the loose gravel in the road grips at my knobby bike tires, and there's a persistent uphill rise I never notice when I'm on foot.

Plus it's hot.

Smoking hot. Jared's house is just about dead centre of this part of the island – a couple of kilometres from the shore on either the north or the south side – and the air is thick and heavy here, away from the river breezes.

My lungs scream, my thighs burn, and I'm sweaty all over by the time I reach Jared's driveway. I stop for a minute, beside the metal mailbox announcing "Strickland," to let my heart rate slow.

It takes a minute to adjust to the silence of no gravel crunching under my tires, and the fading of the noise of blood and breath crashing through my body.

Slowly, other sounds creep in. The perky whistles of the bobolinks. The cicada buzz I never hear by the water, but which drones insistently here. And Rex. Not barking – he never barks at me anymore – just greets me with a gentle whine as he noses his dark wet snout into my palm.

I smooth his ears, and hold my hand out so he can bump the hard brow of his face against it, work a hidden itch against my fingernails.

His ears perk, and he pulls away from me. He trots toward the barn, then stops, looking back, as though to say, *Well, are you coming or what?*

I start, then pause. "Hey, Rex, wait a sec," I fumble my pannier open to pull out the lemon loaf, snugged carefully in wax paper secured with twine, because Betsy doesn't believe in plastic wrap.

Rex waits, but not for long. Lifts his head back toward the barn and sets off again, leaving me jogging in his wake, watching from a ways back as he noses through the barn doors.

My heart's thumping hard again. Jared could be right in there. And if he is, what am I going to say to him? How do I start up a casual conversation when I know this huge thing about him?

I nudge the big double doors open just enough to let me through; I need a few inches more than the slinky dog. Stepping from the beating heat of the sun to the living warmth of the barn is like coming home. Nearly, anyway.

There are a few key differences from the stables I'm used to – the space is less divided, with a row of open tie stalls at the front – but there are still a couple of familiar box stalls, and all barns, no matter where they are, and how clean they are, smell like dust, and like the animals that live in them.

This one's no exception. All barns are cozy. To me they are anyway. To me all barns feel safe, and all barns are beautiful. I don't just love horses; I love all the things that come with them, the components of horsey-living.

Being here reminds me of why I never minded spending a Friday night pulling Major's mane, instead of being at a sweaty, too-loud school dance. Besides, I always thought Major was better-looking, and had better manners, than any guy I'd ever met.

Of course, that was before I met Jared …

I close my eyes, and breathe in the smells of dust, and dirt, and straw, and hay, and peace seeps into me.

"Hey," Jared's voice is warm – barn-warm – soothing, like honey, with his already familiar laugh behind it.

"Hey back. I dig your barn."

"Well, that's something. I guess I always hope girls will dig me for my brawn." He curls up his lean arm, showing a bicep which I'm sure is strong, but isn't exactly *brawny*.

"Or my good looks." He plucks a length of hay from his tangled hair. "Or, preferably for my wheels. You've seen those and, if I'm not mistaken, I think you liked them."

My laugh is intensified by relief. I've never known Jared to be anything but easy to talk to – why was I so worried? "You've got me all figured out. I *do* like your wheels. But I prefer your barn. Hands down it's my favourite."

"And the brawn? And the good looks?"

"Don't go there. Take what you can get."

"Speaking of which, what's that?" He gestures to the lemon loaf I'm holding in front of me like some sort of offering to the barn gods. Instead I hand it to him.

"It's lemon loaf. Betsy's special. Baked this morning with fresh eggs. It's to say thank you to you and your mom for fixing the bike, and the cherry pie, and the ride home."

"Whatever." He drops his gaze. *He can't take a compliment.* I like that. "I want some lemon loaf. Should we eat it in the hayloft?"

"Absolutely. Can't think of a better place."

****

And once we get up there, I really can't. We sit on twin hay bales pulled up against the open loft doors, and swing our legs outside while we munch on Betsy's tart-and-sweet lemon loaf.

"Oh wow, I've got to stop eating this."

"Betsy'll give us the recipe." Jared snags another slice. "We can bake some more."

"Where do you put it?"

"Hollow leg." He taps his jeans. Hard work and lots of washing have faded them into appealing softness. I want to touch them. I reach out my hand, then catch myself. *That's somebody else's body.* The combination of the warmth of the air, and the sweet smell of the hay, and the sugar in the baking have kicked my senses into overload.

Rex whines from the bottom of the ladder, reminding us that we've abandoned him, and he'd like some lemon loaf too, thank-you-very-much. I reach for the loaf. "Should I throw a piece down for him?"

"Don't you dare!" Jared grabs my arm. His hand is warm, and his grip strong, without hurting. A tingle runs through me and my cheeks rush hot. I'm relieved when he keeps talking. "I love lemon too much to waste it on a dog."

I giggle. "I know. Betsy told me just how much you like lemon ..." I freeze. My giddiness drains away. I wish I could back up nine words – unsay them. Or I wish I could figure out what to say next to gloss over the unfinished story about Jared, and his dad, and the lemon meringue pie. *Why am I so stupid?*

"Oh yeah? She told you that story?" He's not laughing, but he doesn't look angry, or upset, either.

"Um, yeah. The one about the church supper? I thought it was cute."

"Well, Betsy's lemon meringue pie is definitely worth stealing."

Phew. My shoulders fall back. I didn't realize I was hunching them. Minefield navigated.

"What else did Betsy tell you?" His voice is light, but it doesn't hold the laughter that's already so familiar to me.

Turns out, I'm actually standing on a mine and I'm not sure how to get off. What would Betsy do?

I take a deep breath. Figure the truth is as good a strategy as any. "She told me your dad died." I pause, breathe again. "I'm really sorry. That's all I can say. I don't know what I would have done if it was me. I'm sorry for your loss." It comes out stilted, awkward, but I truly mean it. I hope he can tell.

He's not saying anything.

I blink at the blue sky, and the shreds of white cloud in it, and Jared's cattle, heads down, grazing in the field, and feel the familiar prickle of hay bales on the back of my thighs, and wait.

"Thanks."

"For what?

"For ... just for what you said. It was nice. It's OK. I mean, it's not OK – it's still hard sometimes – but it's better than it was."

I reach out, half-aiming for his hand and then chickening out at the last minute. I rest my pinky finger about an inch away from his, and lean my shoulders in his direction. "We don't have to – obviously – but if you ever want to talk ..."

He nods. "Let's start with your horse. I'd like to know about him."

"Oh, God, that. I'm so sorry. I feel so stupid that I was talking about losing a horse when you and your mom ..."

His stare makes me shut up. When I'm quiet, he asks, "So, are you going to tell me?"

"Really?"

"I asked."

I clear my throat. "OK, well, I got him as a rescue off the racetrack. He was scared of everything at first, but to other people he just seemed crazy. He'd bite me, kick the farrier, chase anything that came into his paddock. It took two years, but this spring we were really ready. We were going to show all season. And then, at the first show, his heart just stopped – an artery ruptured. We crashed through a jump, and that was it." I tuck the ends of the hay

in, make a neat wisp with it – just like the ones I used to groom
Major with. "It sucked."

"You must miss him."

"It's nothing compared to what you've been through."

"Grief isn't a competitive sport."

"Thanks."

He swings off the hay bale and to his feet, brushing fluffy
yellow crumbs from the creases in his jeans. "So, should we find
you a horse to ride this summer?"

He holds out his hand, and I turn my head on the side and
squint at him before accepting his grip and letting him pull me to
my feet. "Yeah, sure, of course." It's easy to say yes to something
that's never going to happen.

Text from Slate: Cherry pie irrelevant (although delicious).
Is he hot?

Chapter Eleven

I'm stalling. I know I am. Leaning over the fence as far as I can reach, arm extended, clucking and calling for the little pinto horse I've been making friends with during my morning runs. "Hey Paint! Over here!"

I just want to give him a carrot. That's true.

It's been too long since I've patted a horse. OK.

I don't know what I'm going to do for the rest of the day. That's more like it.

It's my day off. Which should be good. Except … it's a long day stretching ahead of me.

And I'm already nearly done my run, and it can't be later than seven-thirty.

I meant to sleep in, but my mind wouldn't still. One of the biggest shows Slate and I were supposed to be going to is this weekend, just outside Toronto. I couldn't stop thinking about it – not the classes, or the ribbons – but of the Tim Horton's stops we would have made on the trip, and decorating Major and Obsidian's stalls to make us all feel more at home, and begging Slate's mom to let us order room service, until she caved and let us eat pizza in bed.

If I was at home, and we were still going, I'd be so busy today; probably shampooing Major, and packing for both of us.

As it is, here, nobody needs me today.

Paint, at least, takes pity on me. He wanders over, pausing now and then to grab a particularly lush mouthful of grass, and finally ends up in front of me, ears pricked forward, tail whisking the flies away.

"Hey buddy, boy." I balance a carrot medallion on my outstretched palm. "Is that good?"

He lips it away, and lets me rub his ears, pat his face. Within seconds, my hands are crusted with black grime. "Man, have you ever been brushed?" He pushes his neck against my scratching fingernails, and I laugh.

"Hey there!"

"Geez!" Paint sends a disapproving noise rattling through his nostrils, and backs up with his head thrown in the air. I whirl around to face Jared. "How did you do that? Where's your tractor?"

He points to it about a hundred metres away along on the shoulder of the highway. "I was patching the fence. I saw you. I walked over."

"You just about stopped my heart." I point at Paint. "And pissed him off too."

"About him ..."

"What 'about him?'"

"What are you doing today?"

I'm suddenly conscious of the sweat beading along my hairline, the possible smell of my laundry-overdue t-shirt. "Um, it's my day off. Wednesday's my day off. And this is Wednesday. So, um, running, and then swimming and then ... stuff."

"Stuff?"

"Yeah, super-important stuff." *Like laundry, maybe.*

He shrugs. "OK, fine. Don't want to interrupt super-important stuff."

"Wait! Why? What would the interruption be?"

He shrugs again. "Oh, nothing really. Just, maybe, something that will help both of us."

"How?"

"I know a guy who needs some help with his cattle. If you can be ready to go in half an hour, he'll give us a day's work."

"And, other than the sheer joy of spending the day with smelly cows, this helps how?"

"He's got a horse. It was his daughter's, and she's moved away. I hear he wants to get rid of it. Maybe swap it for a day's work?"

I raise my eyebrows. "*Sure ...*"

"Great, that's good."

I open my mouth to explain my "Sure," meant "Yeah, right," not "Yes, OK."

"What?"

"I, uh ..." *Shut up, Meg.* I was just wondering what to do with my day off, and here's an answer. "... nothing."

The lure of another slice of carrot has overridden Paint's disgust at my earlier outburst. He pushes up against the fence again, and nuzzles at my neck.

"Maybe it'll be a nice horse like this."

I wrinkle my nose.

"What? Isn't he a nice horse?"

Paint whiffles the sugar cube from my palm, and I tease a burr out of his forelock. "Well, apart from only having one eye ..." I smooth my hand over the long-healed bump where Paint's second eye once was, in his younger, prouder days.

"Hmmm. Yeah. Now that you mention it, even I can see that."

"Well, apart from that, he's a pinto. Solid-coloured horses are a safer bet. Judges tend to like them better. It probably sounds silly to you ..."

Jared interrupts, "No: it's the same with cattle. They're judged on their looks too. It makes sense to me."

"What about you, though? The people. The handlers, I guess you call them. Do you have to look good too? Because we do, in riding."

A smile grows on Jared's face. I know that smile already. Something inside me lifts in response to it. "From the looks of some of the people who've beaten me, I'd have to say no."

"Well if you didn't win, clearly handlers' looks don't factor in." Oh my God, am I flirting? At seven-thirty in the morning? Slate's message pops into my head – *Is he hot?* A race of butterflies starts at my toes and flutters up to my neck where I shiver it loose. I break eye contact. "I should get going."

"So, pick you up in half an hour?"

"OK."

"OK."

I move away from the fence, and step back onto the road, ready to take off on my run again.

"Hey, Meg?"

"Yeah?"

"Is there anything worse than a pinto?"

"Oh yeah. An appaloosa. Kiss of death."

"An appa-whatta?"

I strike off running, call over my shoulder, "Loosa!" I yell, "Google it!"

****

I'm ready in twenty-five minutes so, while I wait, I stand in the magic spot on the front lawn of the cottage where I can sometimes get a cell phone connection. I answer my mom's latest text warning me not to run the dishwasher when I'm not home – **Don't worry; not using dishwasher** – then realize that will give her a heart attack if I don't add: **Doing all dishes by hand.**

Next, I thumb a belated reply to Slate. **Hot?** I start, then pause. How am I supposed to describe Jared's relaxed, outdoor, hay, sun, and baseball cap look in a hundred and sixty characters? Type: **IMHO, yes**, and press send just as Jared's truck rolls down the driveway.

"Hey, again."

"Hey, again."

"Morning."

"Morning."

I settle in, buckle my belt, and Jared points at a travel mug leaned precariously against the seat back. "Tea OK? Green?"

"Yeah, thanks, love it."

"My mom said you would."

Once we're rolling down the highway, I take a sip of my tea. "So, what do you get out of this?"

"Pardon?"

"You said it was 'something that could help us both' and then you told me I might get a horse out of it, so what's in it for you?"

"Money."

"Money?"

"It's not volunteer work."

Money is a normal motivation for a day's work, but it seems flat, somehow. "Oh."

"Oh, what?"

I shrug. "I guess I just thought it would be something bigger. Something *more*."

"Fine, then. Helping you get a horse."

"Why would you care about me getting a horse?"

"To make you happy."

My instinct is to giggle, or snort, or say *Yeah, right.* Except he's serious – at least his tone is.

And, so, I leave it at that. Shut up, watch the fields whip by, and sip my tea. *It doesn't really matter. As if I'm getting a horse today, anyway ...*

****

When we step out of the truck, four guys turn to face us. They look me up and down. Jared pokes a thumb in my direction. "This is Meg. She can handle livestock."

A couple of nods, a couple of hats tipped, and it appears I'm in. I sure as heck hope Jared's right; that I can handle livestock to their expectations.

We work all day: hot, dusty, sweaty work. My jeans stick to me, and I can feel the back of my neck turning brown. My farmer's tan is developing nicely.

We settle into a groove; filing cows through a rusty contraption of rails, springs, joints and gates. I stay well away from the levers and mechanisms, afraid I'll pull up when I should push down, free a cow into the field instead of trapping its head to let the more expert cattle handlers do their stuff with it.

The others move around, taking turns doing different jobs, but I stay at the back, driving animals through the chute. Yelling "hya!" and waving my arms, slapping rumps if necessary.

I work mostly with Jared's younger cousin, Will. I'd guess he's about eleven or twelve. He's a small boy with a big grin, and time flies as we work side-by-side, trying to make sure there's always a cow ready to move forward.

"You're not so bad for a girl," Will tells me as we sit in a circle at lunchtime, and Jared says "Whoa, hands off; she came with me."

Everyone laughs, and Will and I both blush.

I'm grateful when Will's dad, Rod, jumps in. "Speaking of hands off, do you know what he did the other day? You know my brand new truck? The one it took me all year to buy? Well, I came in from the fields and it was nowhere in sight. Turns out, that one …" he points to Will whose eyes are wide as saucers, palms up in a 'who, me?' gesture, "… drove *my new truck* to the back barn to collect the eggs, and then forgot he drove, and walked back. I found it sitting there, all shiny in the grass. I could have killed him."

It seems like the forgetting of the truck was worse than the eleven-year-old driving it. *Seriously, not in Kansas anymore.* Jared catches my eye and grins. I wonder if he has any idea what I'm thinking.

After shrugging off his dad's story, Will nudges me. "You wanna work together again after lunch?"

Jared leans over, tips his cousin's hat over his forehead. "You'd better watch out. Next thing you know he'll be trying to take you home."

To which Rod graciously speaks up, "And most welcome she'd be too," which brings lunch to an end, and sends us all back to work.

The sun's shadow is starting to lengthen as we file the last cows through. I've done the exercise equivalent of about four runs, and it's a bad sign that hidden muscles are already starting to sing. What'll happen when they stiffen up?

Just before they climb in the truck, Will asks his dad something and, getting a nod, runs over to me. "We have a big barbeque every summer. It's coming up in a bit. Dad says I can ask you to come. Will you?"

I laugh. "Sure. Probably. Thanks."

Will runs back to the truck, and Rod yells, "Jared knows all about it. Hope to see you soon!"

I turn back to Jared to ask "What's all that about?" and he's gone.

"Jared?" I spin in a full three-sixty and spot him talking to Tom, our boss for the day.

"Hey, Meg!" He waves at me. "Come on over here. We need to go see this horse!"

The horse. Of course. I'd put the horse at the very back of my mind. It was a bizarre idea. Nothing would come of it. In my world, horse purchases are carefully planned, involving appointments and commissions, vet checks and two-week trials. Horses cost a lot of money. Nobody just says, "Hey, thanks for helping with my cows, can I interest you in a horse?"

This is crazy. I smile and walk over to Jared and Tom. *Crazy.*

Tom points her out in a field that slopes down to the river. She's standing in the middle of a herd of cows and a donkey.

He whistles and her head flies up, ears pricked in our direction. She's black with a bright star and a tiny snip on her face. Her ears, outlined against the blue sky, have a slight inward curve. "She's nice-looking."

"I don't claim to know much about horses, but I think she is. I can bring her in if you want a closer look at her."

Jared speaks up. "Sure, that would be great."

As Tom unhooks the chain on the gate, a current of activity runs through the herd. The cows shift, leaving the mare in full view. I suck in my breath.

"What is it?" Jared asks.

"Remember you were asking me what an appaloosa is?"

"Let me guess. She's one."

****

We're driving home from our long day of work with the appaloosa in a trailer behind us.

I pinch a fold of skin at my wrist. *This cannot be true*. But a quick glance in the rear-view mirror shows Tom's trailer – borrowed for the trip – behind us, bumping and rattling over the rutted road.

Her name is Salem. She's seven or eight. Maybe. Tom's daughter used to jump her. He has a pile of jumps in one of the barns at the back of the property that he'll give us in return for another day's work.

"He's scamming us, you know," says Jared.

"Pardon me?" I pull my gaze from the mirror to look at Jared.

"It's just Tom's way of getting more work out of us. He doesn't have any use for those jumps. In fact, they're taking up room he could use for something else. But there's no way he'll just give them to us when he can get another day's work out of the deal."

"Oh, that's OK. I don't mind. Jumps are really expensive." I shake my head. "Sorry, unless you don't want to have to deal with getting them. I totally understand. It's no big deal."

"Meg?"

"Yeah?"

"Shut up. I'm happy to get the jumps."

"But not today. I'm really, really, ridiculously, completely tired out."

"Can't tell."

"Really?"

"Well, maybe a little, but you did good. Will's right; you're not half-bad, for a girl."

I swat at his leg, and he protests, "Watch out, I'm pulling valuable cargo!" and I go back to gazing in the rear-view mirror and wondering how, exactly, this all happened.

Chapter Twelve

As I run the kinks out of yesterday's work-stiffened muscles, I'm half in denial that Salem will actually be there, in Jared's field, where we turned her out last night. The day's grey, with clouds so low they almost meet the drifting fog, to form a wispy, shifting curtain. It fuzzes the landscape and swallows trees, barns, fences. It distorts sound, so that a truck passing on the highway sounds closer than the cow lowing next to me. In this unreal landscape it's not a stretch to imagine Salem as a ghost horse as well; an unlikely figment of my imagination.

She's not, though. She's alive and real. Pacing the fenceline. Wearing a path in the long grass. Whinnying long and hard when she sees me. Nostrils flared, sides heaving. "It's OK." I slip her a carrot. "You're fine." I pat her neck, and clouds of dust rise from her coat. "You need a clean-up, don't you?"

She is so not Major. She's shorter, stockier, *spottier*.

She snorts, tosses her head. I don't like the way she's pacing. "Just a sec." Tom threw half a bag of sweetfeed in with Salem. In fact, jumps aside, I thought he was quite generous. He also handed over a bridle, a bareback pad and several brushes.

I reach into the feed bag, load a good scoop's worth in my t-shirt, and, with grain dribbling out behind me, duck through the fence and over to the big tree in the middle of the field. I hold my hem out and spin, and sweetfeed flies out all around me in a big circle.

It doesn't take long for Salem to come nosing over to see what I'm doing. I slip her a palmful of feed I saved and, as she crunches it down, I point her nose at the ground.

I leave her whiffling through the grass, searching out the tiny grains with her dexterous muzzle.

On my way back past the field, she's still nose-down, wandering. I don't slow down – I'm glad she's distracted – I'll see her this afternoon.

The morning continues sombre and unsettled, with showers sweeping in from the river, racing across the fields. I time my run up to the B&B between downpours.

When I step inside, Betsy has a message that throws me even more off balance.

"Your mom called yesterday afternoon. She has meetings in Toronto; she's going to stop here overnight on her way."

"Oh." This, perhaps, is not great timing.

In a way, I'm in good shape. I vacuumed last night. Of course, it was mostly because I tracked dirt across the floor when I came in from working the cattle all day, but my mom doesn't need to know that. She'll just see the fresh vacuum tracks on the area rugs and, even if I haven't done as good a job as she would, the cottage as clean as I can make it.

Still, tidy cottage or not, I have this funny feeling it would be better for my mom not to know about Salem just yet. She might not understand.

I hardly understand.

I smooth the sheets on the bed in the front room, looking out over the meadow. I have to check on Salem this afternoon. Everything at Jared's is still new to her. But how much time will I have between work and my mom's arrival?

I plump the pillows. Should I tell her after all? It might be easier. *No. Bad idea.*

Arrange fresh towels neatly on the towel rail. And if I'm not telling *her*, I probably shouldn't mention it to Betsy just yet.

I scoop up the dirty laundry and carry it downstairs. Is the cottage clean enough? The cottage, my mom, Salem ... a headache pinches at my temples.

"Meg? Meg! What do you think?"

"What? Sorry! Pardon, Betsy?"

"I've asked you three times if you want to have dinner up here with your mom tonight."

"Really?"

"Of course. Your mother will be exhausted after working all day and then driving here. She won't want to cook. You can help me put a nice meal together this afternoon and we can all eat here when she arrives."

"I ... oh no ... look!" I point at fresh raindrops dotting the windows. "I'll get the laundry! And, yes, please. Thank you. Dinner here is a great idea!"

I yank the sheets off the line under a spattering of fat drops. Later, I end up caught in the chicken coop, tapping my foot as a sudden sweep of hard rain drums on the roof.

In and out, in and out, the showers blow back and forth across the B&B all afternoon while I check my watch. When can I go? When will this rain end? How soaked will Salem be?

As I finish folding the last of the line-rescued laundry, the heaviness has lifted from the air, and it's been long enough since the last downpour that the surface of the gravel is drying to a light grey.

"Off you go." Betsy says. "You obviously have something on your mind. We've got the food prepped. Dinner at six-thirty?"

"See you then!"

****

I push through the final invisible, killer rise up to Jared's driveway, standing on my pedals, using all my weight to thrust my bike forward. I prop it against the fence by the mailbox and go to find Salem.

Fifteen minutes later, I'm still looking for her. I called at the gate. Nothing. Shook a bucket of sweetfeed. Snapped a carrot. Both of these noises are almost certain to start a stampede with most horses. Still no Salem.

Maybe Jared put her in the barn. But when I step inside, the barn's empty. The air's quiet and close – like a church. Things scuttle in the corners, but they're much smaller things than an appaloosa mare. I climb up to the hayloft and scan the fields in all directions, as far as I can see. No black and white spotted bum anywhere.

I kick a bale of hay, and a barn cat scrambles out from behind it. "Sorry girl, but if I don't find that damn horse soon, I'll have to head straight back to Betsy's."

I'm just dropping back down from the waist-high bottom rung of the hayloft ladder when Jared walks in.

"Hi," he says, slow and with a smile in his voice.

A smile grows in me in response. "Hi, back."

"What's up?"

I hold up the worn lead shank Salem came with in one hand, my carrot in the other. "Oh, you know, I have this little thing called a horse to look after."

"You like her?"

"Sure. Yes. Of course." Not that I know what I'm going to do with her, but the way he's waiting, smiling, I know "Yes" is the right answer.

"So, can you show her?"

I have no idea. Don't know a thing about her. Don't even know if I want to show again. I smile. "Probably."

"Great!"

"But I definitely won't be showing her if I can't start working with her."

"What do you mean?"

"I've just spent ages looking for her. I have a feeling I'm going to feel kind of stupid when you tell me where you've put her."

"Damn!" He drops the pitchfork he's holding and power walks out of the barn.

"Jared?" I follow him. "Jared? What is it?"

He climbs up on the bottom rail of the fence, tugs his baseball cap down low over his eyes, and scans right to left. "Damn!" He drops down, strides over to the truck, opens the passenger door and sweeps his arm wide. "Hop in. We'd better start looking."

I narrow my eyes. "Is there something I should know?"

He shifts from one foot to the other. "Don't waste time. Just get in."

As soon as he settles onto the seat beside me, I try again. "Is there, perhaps, a reason your friend Tom was so willing to get rid of Salem?"

He turns the key, and the truck rolls forward, accompanied by the crunch of gravel compressed under rubber.

Jared glances at me, then looks left as we turn onto the road. "I thought it was his fences. Tom's not exactly the most careful guy. He doesn't keep his place in the best shape. He said she was a runner, but I figured she more wandered away than ran. And, anyway, he said she hadn't done it for ages. He figured she'd grown out of it."

"Great. Fantastic." I had a horse for a little while.

We're heading south, toward the highway. Behind us, the road travels through more fields, then an orchard, and finally peters out into a makeshift ramp leading straight into the St. Lawrence. Ahead of us runs the blacktop. "How do you know which way to go?"

"I don't. But if she's gone the other way I'm not too worried."

Whereas if she's gone this way, you are. No point saying it. I jam my hands under my thighs, lean forward, and squint at the horizon.

Horse. Highway. Cars. My chest tightens, with my heart thrumming too loud, too hard, against the underside of my ribs. I usually feel this way in the middle of the night; reliving the accident I can't go back and change. Only that's in the past. This is here, now, and the pressure's on to make a difference this time.

We turn onto the asphalt and Jared scans one side while I watch the other. We cruise along slowly, go as far as the first curve of the huge S-bend the highway takes on its way into the village. He brakes, then sweeps the truck in a broad U-turn and heads back. I grip the edge of the seat, my fingernails sinking into the vinyl underside. *What if she's just a little further on?*

At the same time I'm rocking in my seat – *What if she's back this way and we wasted all this time?*

I'm glad Jared's driving, taking control, making decisions. The clutter in my head would never let me do it.

We speed along the section of road we've already covered, then slow as we pass the turn-off to the Old Concession Line into fresh territory. *Concentrate. Look hard.*

Jared checks his watch.

"What time is it?" I ask.

"Five-twenty-five." The time pressure I thought I was under for my mom's visit seems like a joke compared to this.

The ferry could already be docked. A surge of cars will whiz by here any minute now, driving fast, determined to get home after a long day on the mainland. Not expecting to see an appaloosa mare in the middle of the tarmac. One of them could even be my mother's car.

I shiver at the possibly disastrous results for both horse and driver.

Jared keeps driving.

We come to another sharp bend and he slows, negotiates a second wide U-turn. "I think it's time to start making some calls." He fishes his phone out of his hip pocket and hands it to me. "You call while I drive. I'll give you some names."

"Let's call Carl first." I'm too nervous to talk to a stranger. Carl is solid. Carl knows everyone around here. Carl would be a great dad to have, and neither Jared nor I have a dad we can call right here and right now.

Jared nods. "OK, I'll start driving that way. Maybe he can help us."

My fingers fumble, and I have to clear the number and start again. "Crap!"

Re-thumb it and Betsy picks up on the second ring. "South Shore B&B!" The carefree happiness in her voice catches me off-guard.

"Betsy! We need help. Jared and I are looking for a horse. A loose horse. We're worried she might be on the highway."

Jared touches the brakes and I glance up. A hundred feet ahead, under a shade tree by the edge of the road, is a large shape. Hope lifts my shoulders. Jared creeps forward until the shadow resolves into better view. I shake my head. A horse, alright, but not Salem and not loose. There's a hard-to-see barbed-wire fence between it and the road.

"Sorry, Betsy what was that?" I'm pushed against the back of the seat as Jared picks up speed again. "I missed what you said."

"I asked if it was the black horse with the spotted bum."

"What? How do you know that?" I'm only half paying attention as I continue to scan the fields.

"I'm looking at her."

It takes a minute for the words to sink in. "Stop!" I yell to Jared, and he brakes, throwing us both forward toward the dash. "No, wait, sorry, I don't mean stop, I mean go! Go to Betsy and Carl's!"

Betsy's talking again in my ear. "Not here. Up by the turn-off to the cottage. I've just spotted her through the binoculars. Your mother drove up, and the first thing she said is 'There's a horse loose on the road.'"

"My mother?" *My mother.* "Shit!"

"What is it?" Jared asks.

"Nothing. She's actually straight ahead. We should see her any minute … there she is! … Thanks Betsy. We've got her." I hand the phone back to Jared as I swing out of the truck. My legs are weak with a combination of relief and dread. Just because she's here doesn't mean she's OK.

I hold my hand up to tell Jared to hang back a minute.

Walk slowly. No blood that I can see. *Don't spook her.* Nothing wound around any part of her body. *Don't send her off again.* All four legs on the ground, bearing weight.

I exhale and my whole body responds – blood pumping, heart thumping – which is how I realize I've been holding my breath far too long.

After all that, her "capture" is a major anti-climax. I walk up to her, lead shank behind my back, and she reaches out and noses her muzzle into my outstretched hand. I click the rope on, and she's caught.

"Oh, you!" I cup her jaw in my hands, and press my face against hers, then step back and run my hands over her unmarked neck, down her sound legs. She's fine.

"Are you OK?" Jared's beside me. "You're shaking."

I leave one hand on her shoulder, and turn to face him. "It's just that ... after what happened to Major ... I was a little freaked out."

Jared blinks twice, then nods. "Yeah, things like that stick with you."

"Exactly. Which is why I'm so glad she's OK."

"Me too." He gives her a tentative pat. "Now, what are we going to do with her?"

Euphoria surges through me. No longer preoccupied with Salem's imminent death or maiming, my brain floods with half-formed ideas about how to handle her running away. "Well, for tonight, I'm thinking keep her in the barn. Let me look into it – Google some things, read some forums – and maybe I'll have some ideas by tomorrow."

"I kind of meant now. Should I go get the trailer?"

"That depends. Is the bridle Tom sent over with her still in the back of the truck?"

"You're not going to ride her ..."

"Why not?"

"Because you never have before, and she just ran away, and you don't know anything about her."

A long answer tumbles around in my brain. A long boring answer. I shake my head to clear it, look Jared straight in the eyes and say, "I'm good at this."

Jared leaves me holding a still-grazing Salem. Comes back from the truck with Salem's very dirty bridle, and the biggest, clunkiest-looking helmet I've ever seen.

"What on earth is that?"

"This is the helmet I keep back there in case I ever need to hop on an ATV."

"It's huge. I don't even think I can hold my head up under it."

He holds it out in front of him. "It's a deal-breaker. You don't have to ride her, you know. I'm sure it wouldn't take that long to lead her home ..."

"God, you're worse than my mother." Which reminds me to walk Salem about twenty feet to the right; just to where a huge pine tree obscures our view of Betsy and Carl's and, presumably any view they – and my mom – might have of us.

When Jared follows with the helmet, I take it, jam it on my head. It's ten degrees hotter inside. It covers my ears. Mental note: *Get riding helmet out of shed and bring to Jared's.*

"You look so cute!"

I stick my tongue out. "Can't hear you!"

It takes thirty seconds to slip the bit between Salem's teeth, and the brow band over her ears, then I bend my leg at the knee, with my calf out behind me. "Here, leg me up."

A mumble reaches me that sounds something like, "I don't like this ..."

"Trust me. Lift on three. One, two, three ..." It's as ungracious as most first-time leg-ups are. Jared's not sure what he's doing, and we don't have any established rhythm between us. He doesn't lift until a beat after I say "three." Salem sidesteps away from our ineptitude, and I'm in danger of sliding right back off again, until Jared plants his hand firmly on my butt and hefts me into place.

I sit up, gather my reins, and straighten the ridiculous helmet. "Good. That's done." I resist the urge to smooth my own hand over the still-tingling place on my backside where Jared's rested just a minute ago.

"Let's go girl." I squeeze her gently, cluck lightly. She steps into a willing walk and we're off, heading up the driveway toward home.

It's been ages since I've ridden bareback, and I've forgotten the sheer pleasure of having such a broad, warm surface beneath me: living, breathing, moving hair over skin, over muscle.

I've also forgotten how bony a horse's withers are when you hit them wrong. That comes back to me when I cluck Salem up into a trot, and she leaps forward, sending me into an uncomfortable series of bumps and bounces.

I take a deep breath, let go of the tension built up during our runaway horse hunt, and a change sweeps through both of us. Salem lowers her head and reaches for the bit. With each step originating from her strong hind quarters, her strides are long, powerful, smooth.

My hips loosen to absorb her motion, and my elbows soften to follow her mouth.

This is why I ride. This is what being on a horse can do. Together we are more beautiful than we could ever be apart. "Pretty girl." Her ears flick back, then forward again, as she puts an extra degree of arch into her neck.

Jared creeps along behind us all the way up the long gravel road. He hangs back as we cross the highway, and stays several paces to the rear, driving more slowly than I thought a motorized vehicle could move. I think *light* and *forward,* and Salem responds with an eager leap into the canter.

The length and scope of her stride surprise me. She eats the ground; the fence posts blur in my peripheral vision.

A whoop of joy races through me, filling my lungs, lifting my shoulders. I lean forward against her neck and loosen the reins, whisper "Go! It's OK!" I grip a hunk of her mane and it's a good thing; she jumps forward into a thrumming hand gallop.

She may be shorter and thicker than my old thoroughbred, but she's also quicker. Major was sweet to work with, bold and scopey over fences, but you'd never know he started life on a racetrack. This mare has twice his run.

I rub her neck, give a single cluck, and she digs in deeper, gives an extra surge of speed.

When I pull her up, she's prancing and swishing her tail, and I have tears drying on my cheeks.

Jared coasts to a stop beside us, shaking his head. "Was that really a good idea?"

"Seemed like one to me." The shine in my eyes must be contagious, because his face softens into a smile.

Jared pulls the truck forward, and I slide off Salem. Unlike riding with a saddle, dismounting from bareback feels like the severing of a bond. It always takes my body a minute to return to the state of just being me, having two legs instead of four.

Salem turns and pokes me with her nose. I rub her muzzle. "Good girl."

The seams of my shorts are dark with grime. My legs are filthy. This horse needs a scrubbing. "Tomorrow." I wish I didn't have to leave right this minute to get back to Betsy's for dinner. Wish I didn't have to explain the horse situation to my mom. "Top to bottom tomorrow, OK?"

I lead her to the barn. To where Jared's just getting out of the parked truck. Stop in front of him. "So, what I'm wondering is, how are your fences?"

When Jared draws his eyebrows together and wrinkles his nose, I add, "Not like Tom's, I assume. No missing fence poles or loose rails?"

He shakes his head. "No way. Absolutely not. I check them all the time."

"Then how did she get out?" Before he can answer, I continue. "I'll tell you what I think. I think she jumped. And, strange as that may sound, I actually think that's a very good thing."

Chapter Thirteen

I t's only thanks to Jared acting as my personal chauffeur that I'm able to slip into Betsy's kitchen at six thirty-seven. Not too bad, considering.

Almost-clean yoga pants, grabbed in two minutes while the pick-up truck idled outside, cover my dirt-covered legs, but there's no time to deal with my helmet hair.

"Just drop me here," I tell Jared when we reach the B&B's mailbox. I'm already out, turning to slam the door behind me, when I remember. "Oh, and thanks!"

The screen door creaks when I yank it open. "Hi everyone. It smells great in here, Betsy! Hi, Mom."

My mom's nose wrinkles. "You smell like horse."

She doesn't mean 'you smell like horse;' she means 'what the hell are you doing with that horse?' but I'm not sure what Betsy's told her, and I'm not ready to go there just yet. "Mmmm … yes, well, we had to take Salem – that's the horse you saw on the road – back to the barn."

"Is everything OK?" *Bless you Betsy* ...

"Yes, fine. Everything's fine. And I'm starving. Let me help you get everything on the table."

I avoid looking directly at my mom until we're all sitting down, and then I see Betsy was right about her being too tired to cook. She has dark smudges under her eyes, and tells us about an accident on the 401, a line-up back to Ontario Street at the ferry dock. Betsy pours her a glass of wine, and Carl puts a steak on her plate, and we all help ourselves to three kinds of salad, and fresh bread.

My mom pauses, food untouched, fingers resting on her fork. "So, Meg, about this horse ..."

Betsy speaks up. "I'm sorry to interrupt, Emily, but I'm sure Meg will tell you all about that later. It's been so long since we've seen you, Carl and I were hoping to hear how you've been doing."

My mom hesitates, then nods. "You're right, Betsy. Meg and I can talk later." She looks at me and raises her eyebrows, before repeating, "Later."

I prepare for a tense, polite meal haunted by the prospect of "later," but my mother surprises me.

She talks between bites about cases she's working on, and the implications for her company, and the opposition from other companies. She describes the people she meets with in Washington, and New York, and makes them sound funny. The woman who won't sit down in a meeting until she cleans the table in front of her with a Lysol wipe. The man who brings updated photos of his miniature poodles to each meeting.

I chew on a piece of tender steak, barbequed to perfection – island steak, Carl tells us – and watch Carl smile, and shake his head while he listens to my mom's stories. See Betsy lean back in her chair and grin. Notice my mom's shoulders loosen, her eyes sparkle. I remember Slate's mom telling me, "Your mother is a hoot," after they'd been to some fundraising dinner together. I'd said a polite "Oh, yes?" and silently wondered how much wine Slate's mom had drunk. Maybe she wasn't crazy, though. I guess my mom can be funny.

She pauses to swallow a mouthful of tangy salad made of new potatoes, sun-dried tomatoes, and chives fresh from Betsy's garden. "This is delicious, Betsy. Better than anything I've tasted in any restaurant for ages."

"Oh, that salad is Meg's." Betsy reaches over and squeezes my wrist. "She just threw the ingredients together. The only potato salad I know how to make is the old-fashioned kind with mayonnaise, but I like this one much better."

My mom turns to me. "Really, Meg? You made this?" Her eyebrows are so high they lift her hairline. *Thanks for being so shocked, Mom.* The words are right there, and if it had been just her and me eating dinner alone, I would have said them. But I look at Betsy beaming with pride at the salad I made because I don't know how to make the kind with mayonnaise, and Carl who helped cook this meal after a long day of work in the gardens, and I just nod. "Yes. I'm glad you like it."

Betsy gives my wrist another squeeze and then winks at me. "Anyone for rhubarb pie? Meg picked our first harvest of the season this afternoon."

****

After dinner, I walk down the path to the cottage while my mom drives the car around by the road. I wait in the driveway so I can grab one of her bags.

We clump along the porch and, as soon as we get in, I set her bag in the hall, yawn, and stretch. "I'm tired. And stuffed. I think I'm going to head up and read in bed."

"Not so fast, Meg Traherne."

Busted. I pull my foot, already planted on the bottom step, back to the floor. And wait. *Don't fidget. Don't sigh.*

"Since when do you have a horse?"

I keep quiet on the grounds that I don't believe how long I've had Salem is what's really bugging her.

I'm right.

"And where did you get this horse? How are you paying for it?"

"Her."

"Pardon me?"

"She's a mare. *Her.* Sorry. Just saying."

"Why do you have a mare? You don't even like mares."

I don't particularly like appaloosas either ...

"What are you going to do with her? What's going to happen at the end of the summer? And Betsy says some guy is boarding her for you. An older guy. Who is he? Why would he do that for you?"

That does it. Restraint gone. Mouth open. "Maybe because he *likes* me, mom?"

She stamps her foot, opens her mouth to use this ammo I've just given her.

I jump in, fast. "Not *likes* me, likes me. Likes me as a person. Wants to do something nice for me."

"Why ...? What's ...?" She starts and stops several times.

I throw my head back, stare at the ceiling for a minute, then look back at her. "Listen, Mom. I get it. This is all a bit unexpected. It was for me too. But things are different here. Having a horse here is kind of like having a cat at home. So think of it like Jared's keeping a kitten for me. And, we just picked her up yesterday, so I don't have exact, detailed plans yet, but probably something like school her, and maybe take her to a show, and then sell her for a bit of profit."

"And Jared's just a very nice person, with a very nice mother, and I'm sure if Betsy told you about him, she also told you she likes him, and I'm sincerely hoping you trust Betsy's judgment in people because she likes me, and she likes you, too."

My mom tilts her head to the side, then sighs. "Anything else?"

"Well, now that I have her – Salem – I could use my saddle and some of my other riding stuff from home, but from your reaction, I'm thinking you're probably not interested in getting those to me."

She stoops, picks up her work bag. "It's been a long day, and I have quite a bit of work to get through. So, let's both sleep on this and we can talk in the morning. OK?"

I wait until she's taken a couple of steps toward her room before I mutter. "Nothing I'd like better."

The floor creaks and she turns back. "Meg?"

Crap. Now what? "Yes?"

"I assume these sheets are clean?"

"I put them on after you and Dad left."

"Fine, then."

"Hospital corners."

"We'll see about that."

"You're welcome!"

"Good-night, Meg."

It takes restraint not to stomp as I climb the stairs. *Typical.*

I yank my t-shirt so hard it sticks around my ears. "Ow!"

My mother is so wrapped up in her own world – facilitating corporate mergers, earning promotions and bonuses, and spending the resulting money on endlessly redecorating the house – that I just go ahead and do my own thing until …

Where is my nightshirt? Where could it have gone since this morning? I drop to all fours and fish it from under the bed.

… until she notices I'm doing something that doesn't fit her life brand. Like choosing Major: she wasn't happy about him, couldn't understand why I wouldn't just buy the push-button, championship hunter Craig was retiring. Or taking Woodworking as an elective – "Meg, it's hardly relevant to your future plans, is it?" And, now, Salem.

I got to keep Major, but had to drop Woodworking. Looks like Salem's going to be the tiebreaker.

If you had asked me this morning how I felt about the little mare, I would have shrugged. *Dunno,* would have summed it up. Not involved. Not committed. She was a horse. I would always look after any horse that needed looking after. That was about it.

Then we lost her, and my heart twinged, and I haven't felt that for a long time.

Then we found her, and my heart swelled. Ditto.

Now my mom's opposition worms her just that little bit deeper into my feelings. I want to keep her. For now, anyway. She's sweet, and Jared found her for me. My mom shouldn't get to take her away.

I sit on my bed and rub the braid of Major's hair back and forth between my palms. Maybe it's time to find a better place for it. The breeze blows the curtains in, and I walk over to the window. There's an old nail on the side of the windowsill – who knows what it was for – and I push the strands of the braid around it. There. That's good. I can lie in bed and see it, and think of the horses I've loved. Of the first pony I ever rode – sweet little Willow – and of Obsidian, who has a special place in my heart, and of Major – of course – and, now, of Salem too.

Chapter Fourteen

I blink my eyes open after a one-hundred-percent uninterrupted night of sleep. Wow, I'd forgotten how good that feels. Was it having my mom here – an extra body under the roof with me – that helped me sleep right through? I don't know for sure; I just know I'm full of energy.

Which makes it easy to run up and check on Salem before work. She's safe and sound in the stall Jared and I banked with extra bedding for her yesterday, but the way she shifts her weight from foot to foot, and the agitated flicking of her ears, tells me keeping her inside isn't going to work long term.

When I get back to the cottage, my mom's already commandeered three-quarters of the breakfast table. She has a rhythm going: *sip* – from her coffee, *chew* – from her toast, then *swish* – with her highlighter over a chunk of text.

She looks up after a sip. "Good morning Meg. There's a spot for you here." She shifts an encroaching stack of papers away from my cereal bowl.

While I get my cereal, and boil the kettle for green tea, and cut up an orange, she keeps up her *sip-chew-swish, sip-chew-swish.*

Until the second my bum hits my chair. That's when she puts down the highlighter, sits up straight, takes one last sip and folds her hands. "So, should we talk?"

"Yes. Sure. OK." Because, really, what else am I going to say?

She glances at a note-covered sheet of paper by her side. Oh my God. She's prepped for this discussion. Then again, I'm not sure why that surprises me. If I was smart, I probably would have spent last night prepping myself.

Instead, I slept.

She starts. "Meg, I'm your mother, and I only want what's best for you ..." I swallow some cereal and nod. This will go on for a while. I tend to think it's a good thing my mom's not the kind of lawyer who appears before juries in court; I'm convinced she'd put at least one member of each jury to sleep.

I pay attention again when I hear the word "horse" – it means we're getting close to the actual point of the discussion.

"... this situation seems strange to me. I thought if you got another horse, we'd buy it for you. In Ottawa. And you'd keep it at Craig's. Just like Major."

Like last night, with the salad, a retort jumps into my head; *So you thought you'd control it.*

Also like last night, I remember how keeping my mouth shut avoided a blow-up. I could do without a blow-up now.

I don't take another spoonful of cereal, but I don't open my mouth either. Not right away. I shift from one seatbone to the other. Push back on my chair until the front legs lift from the floor.

My mom's lips purse, and it must be killing her not to say what she always does when I do this – *Do* not *rock back on your chair, Meg!*

I settle the chair legs back on the ground and tap my fingers on the table. "Would you like to meet her?"

"Pardon?" She waves her arm like she's shooing a fly away, but there's no fly there. "Meet who?"

"Salem. The horse." Why did I even bother? "Forget it. It's no big deal. You have to go, and I have to work ..."

"OK."

"What?"

"I said, 'OK.' But we'd better go now so we can both get to work."

Why did she say yes? Maybe for the same reason I made the offer in the first place; she couldn't figure out what else to say.

"Um, uh, sure. Great." I reach for her cereal bowl. "I'll just do the dishes."

Even though it would save time to leave them soaking in the sink, I'm relieved when she says, "Fine. I'll get my things together while you do that."

I can only handle so many surprises in one morning.

****

From the passenger seat, I tell my mom when to slow and where to turn. We roll in beside Jared's truck, dusty, and quiet, telling me he's somewhere nearby. When I bang the car door shut, Salem sends out a ringing whinny, cutting through the bird song, and the sighing of the wind, and Rex's happy whining.

It already feels like home.

"This way." I pull one of the big double doors wide and latch it against the barn wall, sending light spilling across the concrete floor. It's clean-swept, as always, with the unused stalls bare and tidy.

My mom steps inside, looks around. "It seems like a nice barn."

I ignore the surprise in her voice. "Jared works really hard to keep it in good shape. It's a big job."

"It sounds like you like him."

"Of course I do. He's very likable."

"Meg, you know what I mean ..."

"Mom. Don't go there." I step toward Salem's stall.

"It's just that you've always been so busy with riding; you've never had a boyfriend, I worry ..."

"Mom! Come meet Salem."

Salem's ears flick to us, her nostrils flare. She whiffles me all over – my hands, then up my arms, then pushes her nose over my shoulder reaching toward my mom, standing a good few paces back from the stall door.

"She wants to say hi."

"You know how I am with horses, Meg."

I shrug. "Suit yourself. I'm going to grab a flake of hay for her."

There are a few bales under the hayloft hatch. Like Jared was throwing them down and got interrupted. I heft them into the end stall, where he keeps the feed, and split one open to separate out a flake for Salem.

When I turn back with the hay, my mom's one step closer to the stall. She has her arm outstretched and Salem's licking her hand.

"She likes you."

"Don't be silly. She likes the salt on my skin."

"Think what you want, but she wouldn't do that if she didn't like you."

The hay I'm carrying overrides any interest Salem has in my mother – salt or not. She noses at it, and I open her stall door, nudge her out of the way, and spread the hay in the far corner of the stall.

As I turn back I hear a squeak. "What was that?"

"What was what?"

"I don't know. I thought I heard something from the loft."

It comes again. *Squeak, thud, thud* then "Hay!" and a bale hurtles to the barn floor.

Jared. My mind races, 'It sounds like you like him,' and 'You've never had a boyfriend.' Did he hear all that?

"Meg? Who was that?"

Jared walks around the corner, shaking hay from his t-shirt. He nods at me, "Meg," then takes his cap off with his left hand, holds his right out to my mom. "You must be Meg's mother. Pleased to meet you. I'm Jared."

I almost don't recognize this serious Jared. If my mom was worried before, she'll be terrified now. He's so handsome it takes my breath away. So grown-up he seems to be a generation ahead of me. If he hadn't been laughing when I'd first met him, I don't think I'd have had the courage to talk to him.

My mom, though, is smiling. "I've seen quite a few barns in my time and I was just telling Meg how impressed I am with how you keep yours."

"Thank you. It helps that Meg always sweeps up too."

She cocks her head to give me a sideways look. "Yes, you're not the only one telling me how helpful Meg is. Betsy says she's a hard worker."

I'm tallying points in my head now. Producing a horse out of the blue definitely put me in negative territory. Betsy's praise helped me back up. Jared's the wild card. Does he earn me points for being polite, and charming – and for looking amazing in his work jeans – or does he lose me points for the exact same reasons?

My mom's not going to let me know now. She looks at her watch. "I'd better go. I need to drive Meg back to the B&B, then get in line for the ferry if I'm going to make it to Toronto for my meeting."

"Oh, I'd be pleased to drive Meg to work."

My mom opens her mouth, inhales, hesitates.

Jared runs his hand through his hair, shifts from foot to foot. "If that would help, I mean. By saving you time."

She purses her lips back together, nods once and says, "Yes, thank you Jared. That would help me, and I'm sure Meg would prefer it."

"Not at all, Mom."

"Don't push it, Meg. I'm not stupid."

I walk my mom to her car to say good-bye. No kisses or hugs. I half-raise my hand in a weak wave and she acknowledges it by brushing my arm with her hand.

"I'll stop over again the next time I'm on my way to Toronto."

"OK. That would be nice." I kind of mean it. The good night's sleep alone made her visit worthwhile.

Right before she closes her car door she says, "I'm glad I met Jared. It was very interesting."

I'd like to ask her more but she probably wouldn't explain, and Jared's coming toward us anyway, ready to drive me to work. So, I settle on saying, "Oh. Good. I think," and then wave as she rolls away down the driveway.

****

Seven hours later I've got Salem slip-tied to the fence for her big clean-up. After establishing that the occasional fly bugs her more than water, I'm soon sloshing away liberally, soaking everything but her face.

When I'm done, she shines. She wanders from one clump of green grass to another, ripping, chewing and then ripping some more. Every now and then she tugs on the lead shank, and I take a few steps after her.

There are few things in life as happy as a grazing horse, and, for me anyway, there are few things in life as relaxing as the job of just following Salem around while she eats.

The low-slanting sun and ever-present breeze have been doing a good job of drying Salem's coat – and a less-great job drying my t-shirt – but it doesn't really matter. Wet, or dry, this shirt's heading for the laundry.

"Did you just scrub all the dirt off her, and transfer it onto yourself?" It's my familiar, joking, Jared again. A Jared who isn't too clean himself, but dirt sits well on him. It makes his skin look tanned. It defines the muscles in his arms.

"Something like that." Even without being able to get a full-length view of myself, I know I'm filthy. Smears on my t-shirt, splatters on my legs, and goodness knows what my half-soaked-and-partially-air-dried hair looks like.

I jut my chin toward Salem. "Feel her."

"What?"

"Touch her coat. See how it feels."

"I don't know anything about horses."

"You'll know."

Jared strides over, runs his hand along her neck. "Oh! Soft! I had no idea."

"Told you."

He backs up, tilts his head, and his eyes travel over her from tip to tail. "She looks great. So, now what? A show?"

I keep waiting for the idea of a show to be interesting. To motivate me. It still doesn't. But it's also still easy to put off. For now, anyway.

"It's not quite that simple. There's some work to do first."

"Like making sure she doesn't run away again?"

"Well, quite a bit more than that, but it's a good start." I hold the lead out to Jared. "Here: you want to hold her while I work on her tail?" I start from the bottom, using my fingers to tease out tangles and the occasional burr twisted deep in the hair. "I had a thought about the running away."

"So did I."

"Really?" I take a deep breath, about to launch into my theory, then a word flits through my brain: *control* – the word I almost tossed at my mom this morning. I exhale. "So, what's your idea?"

"Well, what did you notice about her field at Tom's?"

My pulse quickens. "She wasn't alone."

"Right. She was with cattle and a donkey. So, I thought maybe that's it. Maybe she just needs ..."

"... company!" I can't resist any longer. "That's exactly what I thought!"

"So you want to try turning her out with some of the cattle? I was thinking the weanlings. Maybe having her around would make them feel more secure after being separated from their mothers. What do you think?"

"I think, definitely. I think, yes." I drop Salem's tail, thrust my right hand out. "I think we could be an amazing horse-training team."

He laughs, and takes my hand. Gives it a shake. I look at our two hands, both dirty, with jagged nails and small scrapes across the skin. I think Slate might prefer a good manicure, but to me these hands are beautiful. A tingle runs up my arm, and I look back at Jared's face, and another tingle runs through me when I meet his eyes.

Then Salem nudges our hands, and we laugh, and pull back.

"I'll go herd those weanlings into this field."

"Thanks, great, and I'll finish with her."

"OK."

"OK."

As he walks toward the field, a late-evening ray of sun hits him, picks out the gold in his hair.

I tilt my head, and squint, framing up an imaginary picture I'd love to send to Slate.

Or, maybe, just keep for myself.

Chapter Fifteen

Hard to believe I'm getting paid to sit in the sun on the edge of the ferry dock, and watch the boat come in.

Fronds of seaweed swirl and sway under my kicking feet, with quicksilver fish darting in and out. The last person who waited here dropped a potato chip, and I nudge it into the water; watch the fish swarm it.

I jump as my phone vibrates in my back pocket. I've almost forgotten what it's like to have cell service.

Slate: So, are you dead, or just ignoring me?

Me: Death is an extreme assumption.

Slate: I got a job serving lunch at Restwell. I think about death a lot.

Me: Restwell?!? Slate working in the retirement residence down the road from our school is a mind-stretching thought.

Slate: It's more fun that you'd think. I curled my hair and they said "another girl named Slate works here, but her hair's different." Old people can be funny.

Me: Do you have a polyester uniform?

Slate: Yes, and I rock it, TYVM. Anyway, since not dead, then what?

Me: Working. Running. Taking care of my horse ...

Slate: ??!!??!!??!!

Me: Don't get excited. She's green and / or rusty. Straight out of a cow field. 15.3. Appy. Craig would hate her.

Slate: So? Major Disaster ring any bells?

She's got me there. I smile, shake my head. *Major Disaster*. It seems like a long time ago.

I poise my thumb to text her back when my phone pings again: Crap. Gotta go. Tapioca time! Byeeee!

The ferry engines are churning just metres from where I'm sitting anyway. I hop up and wait while the big boat grinds into dock, and the massive ramps lowers into place. Then I scamper across the temporary iron bridge and smile at the ferry operator.

"Package for Carl Waitely?"

He hands it over. "Say hello for me."

"I will." And, clutching the part Carl's been needing to fix his ride-on mower, I head up to the main street to find Betsy at the bakery, post office, or general store and help her pack her purchases into the car.

****

In the car on the way back to the B&B, Betsy hums along to a floaty piece of violin music.

I lean my head against the window and relax my eyes until the grass in the ditches fuzzes into a green blur, broken by the occasional driveway or clump of tiger lilies.

It reminds me of the time we first brought Major home two-and-a-half years ago. Craig driving. Happy about the four horses he'd chosen for himself, and to show to some other riders who hadn't made the trip. Pleased with the dainty grey mare the other girl in the truck had selected.

Sighing every time he looked at me.

Slate was right. Craig did not like Major back then.

When I looked into his narrow, dark stall I saw a skinny, dirty, horse. When I tried to handle him I discovered he was head shy, and wouldn't let me pick up his feet.

"Stubborn," Craig said.

"Scared," I countered.

Craig'd given me a sideways look reminding me that as a fourteen-year-old girl, I should be scared to contradict him.

But the shape of Major's ears, and the flare of his nostrils, and the way he held his head, had already gripped my heart.

"What's his name?" I'd asked the trainer showing us around.

"Major. Short for Major Disaster." He'd grinned, like he'd thought of the name himself. Maybe he had.

Craig snorted. "I rest my case. No horse with that name is coming to my barn."

It was the only time I'd known Craig to be wrong.

He'd done his best. Pointed to the five other horses waiting to be loaded into the trailer. All prettier. More polite. All with reasonable names. "Lucky Lady," "Gotta Run," "Okee Dokee," "Dare to Dream," "Rhyme and Reason."

But I'd shaken my head. Refused to budge. And Major'd been loaded into the sixth stall in the trailer – although with large conditions hanging over his head. "On trial only." Craig'd made them write it on his bill of sale. "And the vet's going over him with a fine-tooth comb."

"Fine. Whatever."

"And ..."

"What?"

"His name. He'll never be called *that* in my barn. From now on he's 'D Major.'"

"Why does it matter so much?"

Craig shook his head. "Sometimes it's better not to court trouble. A name like that – it makes me nervous."

Betsy slows for the turn off the highway and I jerk my head up. Maybe Craig was right. Some people, looking at how things turned out, would probably say he was.

But for me, Slate bringing up the story does something different. It reminds me how much fun I had working with that horse nobody expected much of. Seeing the potential in an animal that didn't look like much.

It makes me itch to get to work on Salem.

****

Salem now shares her field with a half-dozen of Jared's calves, born late last fall and learning to live without their mothers.

She's calm, head down. She's doesn't graze particularly near to any of the big calves, but neither is she pacing, or whinnying, or jumping out of her field. First challenge solved – I hope.

"Let's get to work." I slip Salem a carrot and lead her to the gate.

Now that she's shampooed, it takes no time to groom her, and she's only found a few burrs to replace the ones I worked out of her tail yesterday. I've got her bridle and bareback pad on in minutes, then snap on the clothesline Jared found me yesterday when I asked for something I could use as a lunge line.

I lead her to the level-looking expanse of grass in front of the house where Jared told me to lunge her. "We're not fussy about our lawns around here."

I stand in the centre of the big space, give her some line, and hope she's done this before, and isn't too lazy. I'm not sure the willow switch I'm holding makes a very convincing lunge whip. I cluck twice and order "Walk on." Cross my fingers. *Let's see what you can do.*

She may be smaller than Major was, but she's well-proportioned, and knows how to carry herself. As soon as I ask her to trot she frames right up, neck arched and hind legs tracking up. She picks her canter up on the right lead first try and, for a few minutes, I just stand quietly and enjoy watching her.

She moves like a rocking horse, and she carries her tail held high, like a flag, so it flutters as she moves. "You'll be nice to ride, won't you?" Her inside ear flicks toward me, then back to the front. Promising: she can listen, and she can focus.

As I watch Salem trot around me, memories come floating back of the slow but steady progress and small victories Major and I had together.

There was the first time I ever got him to pick up a right lead canter – the opposite direction from the way he'd always run on a racetrack.

The day I asked him to back up, and he didn't throw up his head, or half-rear, just kept his nose down and stepped backward.

And then, when I finally decided he was ready to jump, he took the tiny fence at double its height, then bucked on the landing for good measure. Turns out Major hadn't been born to race; he'd been born to jump, and introducing him to it was amazing fun.

I let my eyes relax the way I did earlier in the car. I don't look too hard for details and particulars; just try for a big picture impression of the mare. And the impression's a good one; she has good proportions. She'll look great under saddle. And if she can jump the way I think she can ...

Think is the operative word. I *think* she jumped clear of Jared's field the other day. I need to find out for sure before getting carried away.

I call her in, and she comes eagerly, ears pricked forward. If a horse doesn't like to work, there's not much you can do to change her mind. Her energy is a good sign. "Good girl."

I loop the line loosely around the fence and get to work. I go in search of a stack of milk crates I saw by the side of the barn. Bingo. And, lying with them, some lengths of lumber. Perfect.

It starts as carrying, and ends with dragging, and I'm out of breath and sweating by the end, but I get them all in place to form a tidy little X.

I take Salem back out, lunging both directions in trot and canter. She scopes out the jump the first time she passes it and, from then on, her outside ear flicks to it every time she goes by.

No time like the present. I take a big step forward, letting her move away from me so that when she comes around again, the jump will be in her path.

It's no big deal. It's tiny and hardly solid. If she kicks it apart it won't hurt her. Besides, any horse could clear this. Any horse at all; no jumping experience required.

But how she jumps it will tell me so much. Will she be eager and forward, or will she run out? Will she pick her way over it unenthusiastically, or trip through in a clumsy mess?

Please be good at it. Please like it. Please, at least, don't hate it.

She reaches the point in the circle where she first sees the X in her path. Both ears pitch forward, and stay there. Her nostrils flare, wide and pink-rimmed. I have her in a trot, but four strides out, she breaks into a canter. A forward, long-striding canter. With room left to put in one more short stride, she takes off in a beautiful arcing leap, clearing the X as though it was a four-foot wall, landing with a snort on the far side.

"Good girl! Good girl! Good girl!"

Salem can jump. Next step is to do it together.

****

I stand on my pedals, and the breeze funnels down the neck of my t-shirt and flaps out the sleeves and hem. The bike freewheels down the gravel road. At moments like this, cycling is almost as good as riding.

In a few minutes, when I reach the cottage, I'll remember I'm hungry, and tired, and dirty, but right now I'm invincible, riding the wind, my tears drying on my face as fast as they're whipped out of the corners of my eyes.

Stopping at the highway is a formality. Except once an hour, when the ferry docks, there's never anyone here.

Except today.

I yank on the brakes. The tires bite, and I judder to a stop to let Jared turn off the blacktop onto the road beside me.

His window's rolled down. "How'd it go?"

"Good. Really good. Thanks for the line. It worked perfectly."

"So are we any closer to picking that show date?"

"Sure, closer, maybe." My stomach rumbles and I throw my arm across it. "Sorry. I haven't had dinner yet." I lift my foot back to my pedal.

"Hey. Wait. Not so fast."

"Yes?"

"Speaking of eating ..."

I freeze. What does that mean – *speaking of eating*? I'd almost forgotten it's Saturday night. People go out on Saturday night, don't they? On dates? The hollowness in my stomach now has nothing at all to do with hunger; in fact, I'm so nervous I couldn't eat anything right now.

"Yes?"

"That party Will told you about. The barbeque. I was just over at their place, and I promised him I'd make sure you know it's tomorrow."

"Oh."

"By 'oh' do you mean, 'Great, thanks, and I can't wait to go?'"

I sigh. "More like I'm working tomorrow, and it's on the other side of the island, so ..."

"So, that's why I'll pick you up as soon as you're done work, which I know will be early because Betsy and Carl will be going."

"They will?"

"*Everyone* goes to this party, Meg." He adds, "Everyone *important*, that is. Which is why you're invited."

"Oh!"

He smiles. "That sounded like a better 'oh.' So, I'll pick you up tomorrow around four?"

"That sounds early."

"It won't be – trust me – if you're still working at four, I'll personally help you finish making beds or whatever it is you do up there."

"Bring your duster, then."

"I won't need it."

Chapter Sixteen

Betsy comes to find me weeding in the vegetable garden at three o'clock. "Go! Get ready!"

"But I don't need an hour to get ready."

"Well, I do."

"Oh. OK." I put both hands on my hips and bend to stretch out my lower back. Squint up at Betsy. "Wait, should I be spending an hour getting ready? Is this party a big deal?"

She holds out her hand and helps me up. "Don't be silly. You're sixteen and beautiful. I'm sixty-six. You need ten minutes to get ready, and I need ten extra minutes for every decade I'm older than you."

As I'm heading out across the lawn, she calls after me. "But if you brought a dress, this might be a good chance to wear it!"

"Really?"

"Not necessary. Up to you. It would just make a change from working and riding."

Really? I'm wearing the one dress I brought. It's lacy, and light without being fancy, and you'd think that would make it perfect for a Sunday afternoon barbeque, but, as far as I can tell, from my vantage point standing on top of the toilet and bending over to peer in the bathroom mirror (the only way to get anything close to a full-length view in the cottage), it just looks wrong.

And feels wrong.

It needs something to make it country, casual fun, instead of city, tea-party frilly and, whatever that something is, I don't have it.

I glance out the bathroom window – is that Jared turning off the road? *Crap!* Jump off the toilet, run upstairs, yank the dress over my head ... *go, go, go!*

By the time he rolls onto the circular turn-around portion of the driveway, I'm sitting, chin cupped in my hands, hoping he won't notice I'm out of breath.

"You look nice."

"Thanks." My capris and shirt are clean. They're ones I don't ride in, and I feel like myself in them. Good enough.

****

The first person I see when we find a parking spot on the grass, and hop out of the truck, is my cattle-working companion. "Will!" Jared says. "How are you?"

"Good," Will says, but he's not looking at Jared, he's looking at me, and he's not alone. A girl, slightly taller than him, but with the same long thin nose, freckled cheeks, and curling dark brown hair, reaches over and gives him a noticeable nudge.

"This is my sister, Lacey," Will says.

"Hi Lacey. I'm Meg."

"Oh, I know. I hear you jump."

"Um, yes ..." I start to say, but she's not done.

"I started riding Western, but now I want to ride English, and I saved up, and I'm taking lessons in Kingston, but I want to ride at home too, and my pony's a *pig!*" She pauses long enough to take a deep breath. "Will you help me?"

Jared laughs. "That's our Lacey. Little miss one-track-mind. Meg just got here, Lacey. Let me at least get her some food, and we'll both meet you at the barn."

Lacey crosses her arms. "Fine. I'll go ahead and tack Cisco up. You've got ten minutes."

"Wow!" I say. "She told us."

"I'm sorry. You don't have to go."

"No, it's fine. I don't mind at all. She's cute."

"Well I'll come with you, and yank you away before long. Lacey's less cute after ten or fifteen minutes."

I've heard meals called "spreads" before but this one truly is. The food is spread the length and width of a very long, and very wide table. There are salads, and casseroles, and half a dozen different kinds of home-baked bread.

"Hamburger or hot dog?" Jared calls from his spot up by the barbeque.

"Hamburger!"

"Sounds good," says a voice in my ear.

"Betsy! You look like someone who spent an hour getting ready, even though you really didn't need to."

Carl laughs. "I agree with Meg, you look great now, and you looked great before the hour too."

I catch sight of Jared weaving his way over to us, balancing two plates of food. Betsy follows my eye. "I see you decided against the dress." She sighs. "Fortunately, you look very pretty without it, but I do like to see a nice dress."

I laugh. "I'm sure I'll have another chance to wear the dress, but it seems like a good thing I didn't today. Jared's cousin is waiting for me to work with her horse over at the barn."

"Well, you have fun, and watch out for Lacey. She's a piece of work."

When we get to the ring beside the barn, Lacey's riding a slightly pot-bellied bay pony around in circles. Jared leans on the fence. "Alright Lace, I'm giving you ten minutes; then I'm taking her back."

"It won't take ten minutes to see his problem."

Lacey's a bold rider; her aids are strong and decisive. The problem is, her pony – like most small ponies – is also bold, and very decisive about what he does, and doesn't, want to do.

"Watch this!" From an already forward trot, Lacey asks for a canter. The result is an ever-increasing, teeth-rattling pace during which Cisco's legs piston like a sewing machine, and Lacey's head looks like it'll shake right off. They circle three times that way without accomplishing a single canter stride, before I hand Jared my plate, step forward and say, "Whoa!"

Cisco doesn't have to be told twice. He clearly likes whoaing. He stops dead in a beautiful square halt, with his rounded sides heaving from his high velocity trot circuits.

I hold out my hand. "Give me your helmet." Forget the dress, now I'm no longer even going to be wearing clean, non-riding clothes.

Lacey grins at Jared. "I *knew* she'd help me! She's so nice."

Cisco's problem isn't complicated. Both he and Lacey need to focus a bit more, be a bit more disciplined, and all will be well.

As soon as I settle on his back, Cisco's ears flick back, and he works his mouth; sizing me up through the bit and reins. If he's worried I'm going to make him do something he doesn't want to do, he's right.

Jared's laughing. "You could cross your legs underneath that thing." And he's right. Long-legged me, on a thirteen-hand pony, is anything but elegant.

"Well, I think she looks great."

"Thank you Will," I say, then kick Cisco up into a sitting trot. I force him right back onto his haunches, by making the trot as slow as I can without letting him break.

"This is a good exercise, Lacey. See how he'd rather walk?" Sure enough, he breaks for a second before I push him back into the trot. "Trotting this slowly is hard work for him. He has to use his hocks on every step. His muscles are probably burning. You need to sit up straight yourself, and feel out the right pace. Just before he's about to break is perfect." I pause, sense him about to break and give him a nudge before he does. "The key is to keep him trotting, but just barely."

"Then, you can do this." I let the reins out. Start rising in the trot. Release all the forward motion I've been containing. "Let him stretch. Let him ask for the rein. When he sticks his nose out, give him a couple of inches. We want him long, reaching, stretching here. Do you see the difference?"

She nods. Her eyes are fixed; she barely blinks. At this moment Lacey, Cisco and I form a tight little circle of focus and concentration. We're channelling each other.

"I'm going to do it a few more times, and you watch the difference in his gait, his head carriage, whether he tracks up or not."

After several more trips around the circle, both forward and restrained, I say, "I think he's ready now."

I collect him into his controlled trot. His haunches work; each of his hips pushes my corresponding hip up in a mutual rhythm. He's engaged and prepared, so I give him a firm, clear ask, and he pops instantly into a forward, energized canter on the correct lead.

Nice.

"Nice!" yells Lacey.

"Great!" calls Will, and I remember Will and Jared. Hear nothing from Jared. Where's Jared? I bring Cisco back to a trot, then a walk.

"Want to try now?" I ask Lacey, who's jumping from foot to foot.

She scrambles up, while I straighten out my twisted capris. "Where's Jared?"

Will thumbs in the direction of the barn. "Getting something over there."

Lacey's circling by us, adjusting her stirrups. "Just start like I did, Lacey. I'll be right back."

I bump into Jared, coming out of the barn, as I peer in. "Whatcha doin'?"

"Looking for something to measure with."

"Measure what?"

"But I can't find anything, so I'll just have to pace it out."

"Pace what out?"

"Hey, Will, come over here and count my strides with me, so I have a back-up count."

I grab Jared's arm, pull him around. "What do you want to measure? What are you counting? Tell me!"

Cisco, circling twenty metres away, jumps. "Don't let him get away with that Lacey! He wasn't scared for a second."

I turn back to Jared. "Well?"

Will's arrived, and he looks up at Jared with wide eyes. "What?"

"Good question; maybe he'll tell you."

"We're going to make Meg a ring, like this, at my place. So first we need to figure out how big it should be. Is this a good size, Meg, or does it need to be bigger?"

"You're what? You can't make me a ring. That's a huge job."

Lacey veers off her circle and hauls Cisco to a stop right beside me. "You're making Meg a sand ring? Cool! When?"

Jared squints at her from under the peak of his baseball cap. "Soon. I guess if I keep bugging her to show Salem, the least I can do is build her a ring first."

"Showing? Seriously?" Lacey shakes her head. "I'm really surprised you'd want to do that Jared."

"Why? What's the big deal? There are shows up at the community centre every other weekend, aren't there?"

Cisco's using me as a scratching post; dripping warm slobber down my arm in the process. Lacey yanks his head away from me, then turns to Jared, "You're joking, right? You must know that's not the kind of showing Meg does. Those are *Western* shows, with games. She jumps. *English.* You'd have to go to Kingston, or Ottawa to go to Meg's kind of show. You'd have to ..."

"Lacey! That's enough!" I didn't know Jared's voice could drop that deep.

Two bright spots flower on her cheeks. "But ..."

I don't know what's going on here, but Jared's furrowed brow tells me Lacey's about to dig herself into a world of trouble, so I cut her off. "You're not finished your ride, Lacey. Get back out there. I want to see five more good transitions."

Jared watches her go, then turns to cross the ring, counting strides as he goes.

"What was that?" I ask Will.

"That was Lacey pushing, and Jared pushing back. At least that's what my dad calls it. Lacey and Jared have a good fight a couple of times a year."

It still doesn't answer my deeper question of what the pushing was about, but Rod shows up with a beer for him, and one for Jared, and they strike up a detailed conversation about using the harrow and crowning the ring so the water will run off.

Then Lacey leads a very sweaty Cisco over, and she's all smiles, asking if she can help paint the dressage letters. "You see the ones I have here? I painted them. Please say I can paint your letters for you. Please!"

I reach over to unbuckle the girth from Cisco's still-heaving sides, and Jared puts Lacey in a loose headlock and says, "You can't help us with anything if you don't look after your own pony. Take that saddle from Meg."

So, I guess they've made up.

The desserts are even better than the dinner. "There are six kinds of pie here!" I tell Jared. "Oh, wait, no; there's rhubarb too – there are *seven* kinds of pie!"

I chose cherry, and Jared chooses lemon meringue – of course – which works for me because he hands it to me to finish.

"Are you sure?"

"Yeah, I have a tooth that's bothering me. The filling's too sweet."

"Poor baby! Oh well. More for me ..." I worry for a second I've been too flip – too familiar – but he's laughing, so I swallow my apology with a bite of lemon meringue pie.

Jared and I drift around. He introduces me to some friends he grew up with. "There aren't many here, though. Most of them have gone away to university, and they got summer jobs near their schools."

"Do you miss them?"

He shrugs. "I don't know. I mean, yes and no. I miss some of the old times we had together, but everything's changed now, anyway."

"Do you ever visit them?"

He grins. "Yeah, in all my spare time."

"I get it. I know how busy you are, but that makes me wonder if you miss it. You know, school. Having other responsibilities. Being someplace different."

He looks away, and I wonder if he's going to ignore my question. If I've said the wrong thing.

Looks back at me and opens his mouth. Shuts it again.

It's hard to be quiet, but something tells me it's important. The way he blinks, his deep sigh, say he's deciding what to tell me. I want it to be everything, and if I interrupt, it won't be.

"My dad died while I was away."

It's not what I expected. His words send a slap of shock through me.

"I'd been home for Thanksgiving, and just left again, to drive back to school. I figured it out – I've figured it out a million times – it probably happened when I was about halfway there. He was working in a far field – on his own – so they didn't find him until later, after he didn't show up for dinner, and my mom called for help."

I was studying when the phone rang. I drove back in the dark – straight to the hospital – but it was too late."

His voice sounds OK, but I don't think I can talk. I bite my lip and put my hand on his arm. Try a whisper, which works. "I'm sorry."

"So my last memory of school is a bad one. I wish I'd been here, with him, that day."

"And, anyway, I love it here." His sweeping arm points to the wooded area behind the barn, then the fields that slope down to the water. The ever-moving St. Lawrence, with Kingston in the background, and the century-old farmhouse with people flowing in and out of the sliding doors. All this under a flaring pink sunset. "I look at this, and wonder how I could leave."

"Like nothing might ever be the same again?"

He looks straight at me. "Exactly."

"Oh, I know. I get it." My ribs swell as I inhale the scent of a newly-hayed field nearby, the clean smell of river water. "I wonder if anything will ever be the same as it is right now. If there will ever be another Sunday night this perfect."

How did we get to be standing this close? He's got a drink in one hand, and his other one is so, so close to mine. In fact, if I exhale, and lean a bit – just like *this* – I'm sure our hands will brush.

"Meg?" Our hands do touch, and instead of the jolt I expected, there's a slow, warm fizz running through my veins, settling around my knees, weakening them. He encircles my small pinky finger with his callused hand, and the fizz intensifies. *Oh, wow.*

"Here they are, Betsy!"

I yank my hand away, step back into a dip in the grass, and have to take another step to steady myself.

"I thought it was you two over here."

I cough. "Yes, it's us Carl."

"Well, I was saying to Betsy that we might as well drive you home, Meg. There's no need for Jared to drive the extra distance."

"Oh, I don't mind, Carl." *Bless you, Jared.*

Carl waves his hand at him. "That truck of yours drinks enough gas, Jared. Let us take her."

Betsy's caught up now. "Carl, if Jared says he doesn't mind driving her, let him drive her. It's silly to rearrange everything now."

"Well it's arranged now. We'll take Meg. You know I like to help when I can. Let's go!" Carl heads off in the direction of the parked cars, waving at us to follow.

Betsy throws up her hands. "I'm sorry. When he gets an idea, you can't stop him."

My heart rate's slowed and my legs feel steady again. "Oh, it's OK Betsy. He's always thinking of other people."

Betsy walks ahead of us, shaking her head, and Jared comes up beside me. "Is it really OK with you?"

I give him a sideways glance. "Of course not. Carl's car doesn't have real Corinthian leather."

He punches me in the arm. "Next time ..."

I nod. "Next time ..." and I think it as we climb into our separate vehicles, and when Jared pulls off the highway onto Split Oak Road, and after I thank Betsy and Carl for the ride. *Next time. Next time. Next time.*

Chapter Seventeen

T he radio, always on in the background while I do dishes, warned me.

The weather network – Betsy and Carl's homepage on their computer – predicted it.

Even the weather stick attached to the side of the chicken coop said it was coming.

But I'm still not ready for the stifling air I step into after an afternoon spent inside, rubbing at my goose bumped arms, as I helped Betsy rearrange the basement freezer and pantry shelves.

The temperature must have jumped ten degrees since noon.

The super-fine hairs around my face are already curling as I buckle my bike helmet on, and on my way up to ride Salem I struggle to breathe. The afternoon's so humid that inhaling feels like sucking in soup.

While I groom Salem, her dark coat radiates heat. A bead of sweat trickles down my temple. Rex lies on the grass beside us, panting with his whole body; tongue lolling, sides heaving.

"That's it – it's too hot – let's go swimming!" I say. Still no saddle, in the full grip of a heat wave, what better to do?

It's a short walk to the river. I ride Salem bareback, and Rex trots by our side, head down, feet shuffling. Not using an ounce of energy he doesn't need to.

Just before the river, the gravel forks off into private driveways, and the road itself narrows and dwindles into a sort of ramp leading straight into the water. It would be a public boat launch if there was any public around here, wanting to launch boats.

Salem, who's walked willingly forward all this time, slows and hesitates. She halts and lifts a hoof over the edge of the water. *Oh come on.* Please don't tell me water's her weak point.

Rex saves the day. His ears prick forward, and he powers by us – so close his tail brushes the bottom of my foot – and plunges into the water. He wades in up to his belly, circles around until he finds a place that suits him, then sighs and begins slurping.

Salem isn't about to let a dog get the better of her. Her ears pitch forward, and she marches straight into the river, until I'm thigh deep and she, too, is gulping the cool river water, then playing with it, blowing it through her nostrils, and rainbowing sprays into the sunlight.

Once we're still for a few seconds, the sunbeams slicing through the rippled surface of the water highlight lush fronds of green seaweed waving around Salem's legs, with minnows darting around them. A particularly bold one investigates my toes, and I pull my knees up, placing them in front of me on Salem's withers.

Salem wades forward with the water making no noise as it flows around her deep chest. Without my legs to anchor me, I giggle at the sensation of being lurched from side-to-side on her still-dry back. And then, with one step, nothing's dry anymore.

Only Salem's white star and flaring nostrils are still visible on top of the water – those and her pointed ears. Then the power of her underwater strokes kicks in and, with a surge, she rises under me and lifts me through the water. I'm half-swimming, half-riding. I knot my fingers through her floating mane and my t-shirt billows around me.

When she finds her footing again, and pulls us both from the water, we're streaming wet. My clothes stick to me, and her mane's plastered against her neck. Rex looks tiny, shrunken, until he braces his legs wide apart for an almighty shake.

Which, just in time, is my cue to use her withers to push myself up off Salem's back. While she shakes nose to tail, I remember the other way horses like to dry themselves, and cluck her forward to keep her from rolling.

Salem's stride is long and easy as we head back home and, when a swallow swoops too close, Rex frisks after it.

I still have to figure out how to get a saddle for Salem. Still have to hope my mom decides not to fight me on keeping her. Still have a million things to teach her. Still have to try to sleep in this heat tonight, and go to work tomorrow.

But for now, right this minute, I'm focusing on the sun and breeze drying my skin, and the mare I'm riding. I lean forward and pat Salem's drying coat. "I have what I need, right?"

The flicking of her ears means *Yes*. Any good horse trainer could tell you that.

Chapter Eighteen

The heat wave continues the next morning. As I step through the kitchen door Betsy says, "Quick! Close it! The AC is hardly keeping up with this humidity!" She's right. It's cool in here – much better than outside, or in the cottage – but it doesn't have that icy edge of true, deep, air conditioning.

"I'm afraid it's going to konk out, too. The dishwasher died last night."

"What do you mean?"

"Water all over the floor. They can't send a repairman until Friday. Carl's going to pull it out and take it over to Kingston himself this afternoon."

Which means I have to do the breakfast dishes by hand. Unbelievable how many dishes normally slot neatly away in the dishwasher. Cluttering the counter, the sheer number is overwhelming.

I yank my hair into a ponytail, run sudsy water into the sink (why do dishes have to be washed in hot water?) and get to work.

It takes nearly an hour because, just as I'm lifting the last dish out of the sink, Betsy brings in a tray of dirty dishes from the second set of guests' breakfasts.

"Sorry."

I blow a couple of stray hairs off my forehead. "S' OK. This is why you pay me the big bucks."

I've been through three sinks of water, and my hands are like two prunes, when Carl comes in from mowing the lawn. His hair clings to his head, t-shirt is stuck to his shoulders. Maybe doing dishes in (partial) air-conditioning isn't the worst job today.

He throws the mail down on the kitchen table. "Hey Meg, there's something here for you."

"Me?" I assume he means a story in the local newspaper I'll be interested in, or a catalogue I might want to look through. But no: as soon as I've dried my hands, he holds out a slip of stiff card stock.

I take it, read it, furrow my brow, look back at him. "What is it?"

"You tell me."

"It says I have a parcel at the bus station."

"Well, then, I guess you have a parcel at the bus station."

"But what? From who? Who would send something for me by bus?" I double-check: my name on the slip, followed by Betsy and Carl's address.

Carl shrugs. "Your guess is as good as mine."

"Ooooh! Now I really want to know. Do you think they'd tell me if I call?"

He smiles. "Why don't you come over to Kingston with me this afternoon? The dishwasher repair place is up by the bus station. We can swing by."

"Really? You'd take me?"

"I don't see why not. I doubt Betsy's going to want you to weed the garden in this heat, and I'm sure nobody should be doing any cooking in this house."

"I. Am. So. Excited."

"Well, excited, get out of the way now so I can haul this ridiculous dishwasher out."

****

A midday trip into the village, and across to Kingston, means a chance to buy a sandwich at the bakery and eat it on the boat while the scenery of the harbour slips by: tour boats, and batches of bobbing sailing dinghies, and, maybe, a tall ship.

And there's bound to be a breeze on deck.

I run into Jared in the bakery, fishing in his jeans pocket for the extra five cents he needs to pay for his sandwich. I reach across and plunk a nickel on the worn counter.

"There; it's on me," I say to him, and, "I'll have one, too," to the woman behind the cash.

"Don't you get lunch at work?" Jared asks. "I wouldn't be in here if I got Betsy's cooking for free." He tips his head to the woman handing him the sandwich. "No offense, Norma."

"Oh, you couldn't offend anyone, Jared Strickland." She winks at me, and I hope the red in my cheeks can be explained away by the extreme heat thrown off by the big, never-off, ovens baking away.

Matching sandwiches in hand, Jared and I step out of the bakery and into a moment of silence, which we both rush to fill at exactly the same time.

"I'm just going ..." I start, and "Where are you heading?" Jared asks.

"To Kingston." I don't fight my cheeks reddening now; the mystery package hasn't gotten any less exciting. "Carl has some errands to do, and I have to pick up a package at the bus station."

"Oh, yeah? Package?"

"Yup! I'm so excited, I love getting packages, I ... Sorry. I'm a bit obsessed. What are you doing?"

He holds up his sandwich. "Oh, you know, just getting lunch on my way through the village. Then back to work."

"OK, well. I'll be by to see Salem when I get back. Carl's in line, so I should go find him."

"Hey Meg, since you're going over anyway, could I ask you a favour?"

"Of course. Any time." A car rolls past, the first in a long line coming off the ferry. "I've got to get on this boat. Tell me what you need while we walk."

Jared holds up his hand to stop the next car in the convoy, and we dart across. "It's my mom's birthday in a couple of days."

"Oh! That's nice."

"Yes, except I don't have anything for her. And I was wondering if I could give you some money, and you could pick something up?"

As we pass Carl's truck, I knock on the passenger side window and point to the front of the line. Mouth 'See you on board.'

I turn back to Jared. "I thought you were going over soon anyway, to get that tooth looked at."

He shrugs. "Not quite yet. My appointment's later. After her birthday."

"Well, in that case, no problem. Did you order something? Where is it?"

"No. Sorry. I was hoping you could maybe just pick something."

"Jared! I don't know your mom that well ..."

"Yeah, but you're a girl. I mean, don't girls know what to buy for other girls – women – whatever?"

"Sure, why don't you just randomly buy a present for my dad."

"OK, OK. Point taken. She was talking to my aunt on the phone the other day about this new store on Princess Street. I think it's called 'Bluebird.' Maybe you could go there?"

"What do they sell?"

"I don't know – things moms like, I guess."

We're at the edge of the ramp, now, and the cars from the island are starting to roll over it, loading onto the ferry; their tires clanking rhythmically across the overlapping stamped steel plates.

I put my hand on his arm. "Listen. I'll try. If I see something that looks good, I'll get it."

"Really? You don't mind?" He reaches into his pocket again. Pulls out his wallet. "Here. Take this." He holds out a few bills.

I fold them over twice, grip them firmly in my fist. "I'll do my best!"

****

As Carl drives us toward the bus station, I have my hand buried in my bag, where I take turns fingering the parcel notice, and Jared's three twenty-dollar bills.

My stomach flutters every time I wonder what's in the parcel.

It clenches every time I wonder what on earth I'm going to choose for his mom's gift. I exhale. I guess whatever they have for sixty dollars at Bluebird.

But the parcel's first, and definitely the simpler of the two tasks, so as Carl pulls into the parking lot I push gift worries out of my mind.

"The appliance place is just around the corner," Carl tells me. "Are you OK if I head over there and pick you up here in about fifteen minutes?"

"Of course." I point to a small patch of green with a sagging picnic table on it. "I'll wait for you there."

It doesn't take long to get the package, but carrying it over to the picnic table is a challenge.

It's huge.

Not as heavy as it looks, but solid. Nothing rattles as I settle it onto the graffiti-scarred table surface.

It's über-packaged. I can't find a loose end of tape anywhere; every crack is covered with thick layers of smooth plastic stuck on evenly and neatly.

I finally find a paper clip in the bottom of my bag, and unfold it so I can slip the sharp end under one of the flaps of the box. With careful forward slices, I work both flaps free. *Voila.*

I unfold them and my heart speeds up. *No way.*

I think ... but I'm not sure. I reach deeper and feel around. Yes, I'm definitely right. It's my saddle, wedged tightly in place with my saddle pad, and various bandages. And shoved down the side of the box is something I can pull right out. My beautiful, leather halter. With the plaque still on it: "D Major." I pull it to my chest and whisper, "Major Disaster."

My chest aches and swells at the same time. Wow – happy and sad will just about knock you over when they hit together.

I open the note that fell out when I pulled the halter free. It's simple – one of those cards with a running horse on the front, and blank inside – and has big, slashing printing done in bold Sharpie inside. *"Happy Riding, Meg. Love, Mom"*

I sit down to wait for Carl, with one hand resting on my precious parcel and the other making use of the amazingly strong mainland cell signal to call my mom.

"Emily Traherne."

"Mom, hi. It's me."

"Oh, Meg. Why are you calling in the middle of the day? Is something wrong?"

"No, Mom. Nothing's wrong."

"So you're OK? And the cottage is OK? You're sure?"

"Yes, positive. I ..."

"It's just that I'm in a meeting, so if you're fine ..."

"I'm calling because I'm in Kingston and I just picked up my saddle from the bus station."

"Oh. It's there already?"

"Yes. I was so surprised. It's amazing. Thank you."

"Well, I just ..." She's quiet for a minute and I pull the phone away from my ear to check the screen; make sure it's still connected. Put it back in time to hear her say. "I just thought, if you were going to ride, you might as well do it properly."

"I'll definitely do it properly now."

"That's good, Meg. I'm glad."

****

And now for the hard part. Carl lets me out of the car at the bottom of Princess Street.

"I'll come meet you at the dock." I promise. "I won't be long."

I hope ...

Where is this place? "Bluebird." It's a strange name. I hope Jared remembered it right. What if it's a totally different bird name? Or a completely different animal? What if I can't find it?

Oh, wait, here it is.

The floors are natural wood, and the walls are painted blue – not depressing but fresh; calming. I can see why Jared's mom would like it here.

I'm in it, but I still can't really say what kind of shop it is. There are clothes, and candles, and pillows, and soap.

There's too much to choose from in the time I have.

I turn over the price tag on a scarf and cringe. This tiny scarf alone would take all of Jared's money.

I need to get this right.

"Can I help you?"

A woman, also dressed in blue, smiles at me.

"I'm looking for a gift for a woman. Someone I don't know very well. A friend's mother."

"Ah, and you want to get it just right."

I nod. "I want her to be happy." As I say it, I know it's a lie. *I want Jared to be happy with me.*

"Well, let's see ..." She puts her hand to her throat, and I blink. "What is it?" she asks.

"Your necklace. It's amazing."

She lifts it away from her skin – a small silver leaf on a linked silver chain. "Well, that's easy, we have lots more."

She talks as she leads me to the back of the store. "They're all different of course – hand-made from real leaves – but they're all beautiful."

She's right. They are. Simple, and elegant. I love them all, but there's a ginkgo leaf, which looks almost like a seashell, that stands out.

But the price. It's got to be too much.

I point at it. "Could you please tell me how much this one costs?"

The woman flips over the tag, and I exhale. Eighty dollars. Chipping in twenty dollars of my own is a no-brainer.

"I'll take it."

Back on the boat I ease open the bag from the jewellery store, lay the necklace on the seat, snap a picture and send it to Slate: Do you like this?

The answer comes almost immediately: God, yes. One for me please!

So I'm not the only one in the world who likes it.

But it's not important if Slate likes it. It's not even important if Mrs. Strickland likes it. Well, it is, of course, but first Jared has to like it.

What if he doesn't?

Then I guess he should have gone to buy his mom's present himself – it's not my problem.

Yeah, right.

On the way back to the B&B, Carl pulls into Jared's driveway. "Do you need help?"

"No, I'll just be a second. I'll stash the stuff in an empty stall for now, and find a better place for it later."

I leave Carl listening to the weather forecast while I heft the big box out of the back of the truck.

It's strange to be here in the middle of the afternoon, when I'd normally be working. The tractor's nowhere in sight, and Salem and her calf-friends are gathered in the shade of a tree, eyes half-closed, skin twitching against the flies.

In the barn I prop a board across two hay bales, and hang my saddle over it. Carefully snug the cover on, and put the box with the rest of my stuff beside it. Good enough for now.

Now for the necklace. I don't know when Jared needs it, and I figure I should give him as much time as possible to return it, in case he really hates it, so I use a length of binder twine to hang the velvet jewellery store bag from an old nail beside the blackboard by the barn door.

I find a nub of chalk and scrawl: *"As discussed. Hope it's OK. Receipt in the bag in case you want to change it."* I draw a big, cheerful, happy face.

I wish I was as confident as that smiley face. Wish I could just be happy that Jared asked for my help. If I cared less about him it would be easier, but it's too late to care less now.

Chapter Nineteen

I wish I could watch what happened here this morning in one of those cool time lapse videos.

7:30 a.m.: Quiet barnyard.

7:45 a.m.: Truck pulls in. Rod, Lacey and Will spill out of the cab. Jared and I appear to help haul things out of the back.

8:00 a.m.: Rod, Will, and Jared measuring the new ring. Pacing a rectangle, standing in corners, pointing to other corners, conferring, shaking heads, nodding heads.

9:00 to 10:30 a.m.: General blur of activity. Lacey and I painting dressage letters. Jared driving the tractor. Rod pointing where he should go. Will being sent back and forth to the truck, and the barn, for miscellaneous tools.

10:45 a.m.: A huge dump truck rumbles in from out of nowhere. Tilts the dumper, slides a massive load of sand onto the edge of the newly prepared rectangle. Gives a final bang-bang to thump the last bits loose, toots its horn and drives off.

Pause for me to run out. "Who was that? What just happened? Where did the sand come from? I can't believe it! This sand is beautiful. I've never seen so much of it." Me burying my arms in the sand, leading to Lacey and Will burying each other in the sand, causing Jared and Rod to stand back and laugh.

11:00 a.m.: I bring everyone lemonade (it's still thirty degrees in the shade).

11:15 till just past noon: More tractor use. Pushing sand here, moving it there. Mixing it with the top layer of clay soil. Harrowing it.

As the sun hits its highest point – as all of us are sweaty, with rumbling stomachs and a general air of irritability, Jared steps out of the tractor and we all gather around and say, "Wow."

"Is it OK?" Jared asks.

"It's amazing. It's perfect. I can't believe it's here." I throw my arms out wide. "Now I'm buying everyone lunch!"

"What?" says Jared.

"In the village. Pizza, if that's OK."

"You can't!" But he's the only one saying it. Rod, and Will, and Lacey are nodding and saying, "Yes please!" and "Pizza!"

In the truck, on the way, Jared tries again. "You can't buy lunch for all five of us."

"And you can't make me a sand ring in one morning."

"Meg ..."

"I work, Jared. I make money." I point at the truck ahead of us. "They helped me out of the goodness of their hearts. I want to buy everybody pizza."

"You're too nice."

"What are you talking about?"

"You're buying everyone lunch. You bailed me out for my mom's birthday."

It's hard to talk casually, and hold my breath at the same time. "So, the necklace was OK?"

He grins, "She cried. In a good way. I knew you'd make a great choice."

Warmth spreads through me. "I'm glad. I was worried you – I mean she – wouldn't like it."

"I would always like anything you chose, Meg. I like everything about you."

I can't breathe, think, or form a complete sentence. "Oh. Thanks."

Jared pulls the truck over in front of the pizza place. "Come on, let's eat."

My stomach's so fluttery that, for the first time in my life, I'm not sure if I'll be able to eat pizza. *He likes everything about me.*

Turns out Jared's the one who has trouble eating. Will's already started his third slice, while Jared's still working on his first. I catch him wincing.

"That tooth? Still? When are you going to the dentist?"

Lacey mumbles around a mouthful of pizza. "Oh, Jared'll wait for his tooth to fall out before he goes to the dentist."

"Why?" I ask. "Are you afraid of the dentist? Is that what this is all about?"

Lacey shakes her head. "It's not the dentist he's afraid of ..."

"Lacey ..." There's that tone in Jared's voice again.

This time it's Rod who breaks in. "That's enough Lacey. We all have our own particular fears."

"Not me!" she declares. "And I bet Meg's not afraid of anything either."

They all turn to me, and I don't know whose eyes to meet. I settle on Lacey. "Sure I am, Lace. In fact, in the spring, when my horse died, I was afraid of everything. I was afraid my summer would be ruined, and I'd never love another horse again, and I wouldn't be happy for a long, long time."

I shift my eyes to Jared. "And look how wrong I was. Because I met all of you, and I have Salem, and I like every single thing about my summer so far."

****

It's too noisy to talk with the wind rushing through the truck window, so I roll it up. "So, you and Lacey?"

Jared slows as a car turns off the highway in front of us, glances over at me. "Yeah. In some ways she's more like my little sister than my cousin. Which means I love her more ..."

"And she bugs you more."

He nods. "You got it. I know I should be more patient with her. She's a lot younger than me."

I laugh. "I don't think it has anything to do with her age. Do you really think Lacey's going to change as she grows up?"

"You're right. Probably not. And mostly I wouldn't want her to. It's just when she pushes my buttons ... anyway, enough about that, look over there." Jared points to a spot on the mainland east of Kingston, where the sky is roiling grey over mist-like lines of rain. "We're going to get some serious rain. With thunder. And lightning. It's just a matter of when it hits us."

"Well, put your foot down then. I have a new sand ring to try out while it's still dry."

Wearing my matching dark leather saddle and bridle, with her legs carefully wrapped in dark green polos, Salem would fit right in at my old stable – even with her bright, white bum.

Leading her out to the new ring makes this feel like a proper schooling session, unlike the quick ride I took up and down the road yesterday just to try her out with my newly arrived saddle.

The footing feels good under my feet. It has give, without being deep, or sucking. Today is a feeling out day. Our first formal schooling outing. Me getting to know her, getting to know the tack, getting to know the ring; her getting to know my leg, seat and hand. A great big exploration.

I loose-rein her in the walk a couple of laps each direction, letting her stretch her legs and neck, feeling the natural rhythm of her gait. Then gather the reins, sit up straight and push my heels down.

She flicks her ears back, then forward again, and as I'm gathering the reins, she's reaching for the contact. I like her natural head carriage. It suits me, fits where my elbows naturally bend and my hands naturally rest. This is something Major and I disagreed on, and had to work on for months and months. It's something we fought about every time we had a dispute. Finding it working right from the start is a gift. I relax, and Salem relaxes back.

"Good girl."

We spend a solid ten minutes doing walk-trot transitions. The test for her is to respond quickly and sharply. Not surprisingly, she starts out slow and sloppy but, by the end, I just have to think "trot" and there she is, and when I think "walk" again she drops down instantly, but does so without dying; striking out immediately into a forward, reaching stride.

The test for me is to learn her. How she feels, moves, acts. I close my eyes on each upward transition, pick up my diagonal without checking. Don't open them again until I think I've got it right. I start off missing every third one. By the end I'm solid. I've absorbed her rhythm enough to know when it's right, and feel the jar when it's wrong.

She's not conditioned to ring work, so we take a breather before I play an equine version of Simon Says with her. I back up my seat, leg and hand aids with the commands stated out loud. Which makes me sound ridiculous. "Simon says halt!" It doesn't matter if she's not perfect the first time because "halt" will come up again, and again, and again. The trick is, she never knows when. Neither do I. I run through walk, trot, halt. Try "back" and find she's great at that, nearly tripping over herself to back up. It's not just paces either. I ask her to circle: big and small circles, one direction, then another. I keep the commands as random as I can.

"Simon says trot!" It's Jared, standing in the shade cast by the barn over the ring.

We obey. Salem jumps up into a balanced, energetic trot and I rise on the correct lead from the first stride. I take her through the corner and down the long side, and ask her to walk. Let the reins slide long.

She points her nose way out, stretching her neck. I lean forward and pat her from ear to withers, feel the heat coming off her. She's tried hard.

"Was it good?"

I slide off her back, loosen her girth, run up her stirrups. "It was great."

He falls in step beside me as I walk her around the ring. I kick a bit of sand in his direction. "Nice footing, eh?"

"If you say so."

"I do. Speaking of which, where did all this sand come from, anyway?"

Jared grins, looks at me sideways. "I know a guy."

"Do I owe this guy money?"

"You already bought him pizza, and promised his daughter you'd let her jump Salem."

"Yeah, she's pretty persuasive, isn't she? I guess it's a good thing I've already started getting Salem ready for her."

A massive raindrop smacks the middle of Jared's forehead. Then one torpedoes my arm. They're so big, they're visible as they fall through the air around us.

"It's coming!" Jared waves for me to follow him, runs ahead to pull the barn door wide.

The yard darkens like someone's slid a dimmer switch, and lightning snakes through the sky. Salem doesn't have to be told twice to turn and jog beside me into the barn.

We run in just as the follow-up thunder cracks through the air. Rex dekes around the door, tail between his legs, and disappears into the closest stall.

I lift off the saddle, replace her bridle with a halter, and leave Salem cross-tied in the aisle while I join Jared in the still-open barn door.

The rain hammers on the steel roof, and against the sides of the barn. It bounces off the ground so hard it splashes our legs. Tree branches wave and bend as the wind gusts around them. Every time lightning flashes, it forms a different pattern across the sky.

Jared breathes deeply. "Smell that."

I fill my lungs with the scent of lighting-born ozone, and cool air pushing out the heat, and the earth, opening up, releasing everything that's been baked into it by the searing sun. Dirt. Life. Country. Summer.

Jared takes a step forward and turns his face to the sky. I wait a minute, then join him. The constant stickiness of the last two days, the dirt of our morning's work, and the sweat of this afternoon's ride wash away under the steady raindrops.

I close my eyes, and open my mouth, and rain, sweet and soft, courses into my mouth.

And then Jared's hand brushes mine.

I hold my breath. *Was that a mistake?*

He hooks my pinky finger with his.

Oh. Wow. It wasn't a mistake.

My stomach flips, and my breath comes so short and shallow that it dizzies my brain.

"Meg?"

"Yes?"

"What are you thinking?"

How does he expect me to think when he's just laced the rest of his fingers through mine and there's a tingle running up my arm, and trickling through the rest of my body?

I squeeze his hand. "I'm thinking I could stay like this for a while."

His shoulder bumps mine. "Well, I could stay like this until the rain stops."

I lean against him, "Oh yeah? I could stay like this all afternoon."

He props his chin on the top of my head. "Well, I never want to walk away."

Thunder cracks so powerfully I can feel it in my chest, and we both yelp and leap back into the barn.

"Wow!" he says.

"Wow is right." I can still feel exactly how our fingers intertwined. "Wow."

Just before I fall asleep I send Slate a text: **Experienced intensely romantic, hand-holding moment with tractor-driving cowboy. What next?**

Chapter Twenty

Slate: Extreme awkwardness, followed by avoidance and escalating angst.
Me: Thanks, BFF. Your support means the world.

It's my day off, and the heat's broken, and I have all day to ride Salem. She lifts her head, and nickers as I lean on the fence. Rex trots over, and shoves his wet nose in my warm palm, and I flashback to Jared's touch on that same hand. Nice …

Rex is happy with me for about two seconds. Until he whines, and pulls away, and his ears flick to Jared's back, disappearing into the barn.

Rex runs off after his favourite person in the world, and I follow.

"Hi!" I call.

No response. He's in the end stall – the one with all the feed, and the salt licks, and supplements in it. Maybe he didn't hear me.

I walk along the aisle, stick my head into the stall to find him pouring something from a sack into a bucket. "Good morning."

He lifts his hand, and turns his head partway over his shoulder, but doesn't answer. Slate's text flickers into my mind. Please don't let her be right. I hate awkwardness.

I step back from the stall door. "OK, well, I'll be out with Salem if you want me."

"Meg!"

His voice is weird, muffled. Strange enough to make me wait while he sets down the bag he was pouring from and turns all the way around.

He immediately presses one of his free hands against his jaw. His eyes are bloodshot.

"You look terrible."

"'Sanks."

"What's wrong? Why can't you talk properly?"

He points at the side of his mouth. Winces. "Tooth."

"Oh." I step into the stall, under the lone light. Circle his wrist with my hand. He allows me to pull his hand away, but there's not much to see. "How bad is it?"

"S'OK."

But the furrows in his forehead tell me differently. I reach for the bucket he's still gripping. "Leave that here. We're going to go in and call your dentist."

Jared's agitated, and not very helpful.

"Where's the dentist's number?" I'm scanning the corkboard by the phone.

"Mom has it." He shifts from foot to foot. "'Isten, Meg ..."

I cut him off. "Great. So I'll call her."

While I punch in the main number of the big hospital where his mom works, and then her extension, Jared walks back and forth. "Stop pacing," I whisper. "You're driving me crazy."

"Human Resources. Jane Strickland speaking."

"Oh, hi Mrs. Strickland. It's Meg."

"Meg? Is it Jared? Is he ..." The fear in her voice reminds me this is a woman who lost her husband not that long ago.

"He's with me, Mrs. Strickland. He's fine. Except for his tooth – that one that's been giving him trouble – that's why I'm calling; he can't really talk. I know he has a dentist appointment soon, but he needs to go in today."

There's a sigh on the other end of the line. "And has he agreed to that?"

"Well, there's really no choice. My aunt had an abscess, and it was just like this. They're really serious ..."

"Oh, I know, Meg. It's not me you have to convince. I'll be more than happy if you can get Jared to the dentist."

This dentist phobia of Jared's is ridiculous. I should probably feel sympathy, but instead I'm angry. "Oh, I'm taking him."

Mrs. Strickland surprises me by laughing. "Good for you, Meg. You go get in the ferry line and I'll call the dentist's office and tell them you're on your way."

"Great, thanks."

"No, Meg. Thank you. Very much."

"I need your keys."

Still holding his jaw, Jared just stares at me. "I ... I don' wan'..."

"Yeah, well, too bad. I'm a perfectly fine driver. Better than you, in this state. So hand them over. I promised your mom I'd take you, and I'm going to."

Jared makes small noises now and then, on the way into the village, but I don't take them personally. I drive well; as smoothly as I can on the cracked highway. Now that we're moving, my anger's dissolved; I have more patience for Jared's pain, and his fear.

"There, all in one piece." I slide us into the ferry line and put the truck in park. "On the way back you'll feel so much better, we can get an ice cream."

He still doesn't smile, though. Just closes his eyes and leans back.

"Is it that bad?"

His hand reaches out and I meet it halfway, in the air between us. He wraps his fingers through mine and squeezes so hard my bones crunch. But I don't say "Ow" – my fleeting pain is nothing compared to his.

The boat's quiet, with the morning commuters already on the mainland. The traffic in the morning is mostly to the island – deliveries and contractors – they won't start heading back for another couple of trips.

We're one of the few vehicles to load on. I recognize the ferry worker as someone Jared introduced me to at Rod's party – an older brother of one of his friends. He does a double-take as I ease the truck over the ramp onto the ferry deck – must be strange for him to see somebody else driving Jared's truck – but when I wave he nods, smiles and motions me forward.

Jared flinches when the ferry sounds one long blast as it moves underway.

"Do you want to get out?"

A line of muscle tenses up the side of his face. He shakes his head. "Nuh-uh."

I've never seen him so white. His face, and the knuckles on his fisted hand, too.

I remember the thing that comforted me in those long, concussed days after my accident with Major; it was just waking up, or turning around, to see Slate there. To know she was sitting with me. To have someone in my corner.

I adjust the visor to keep the sun off Jared's face. "It's OK." I hesitate, then half stroke, half pat his arm – *you win, Slate; now this feels awkward* – "I'll stay with you the whole time. I'm not going anywhere. It won't take long, and you'll feel so much better."

He gives me a lopsided smile. "'Kay."

"And I'll just shut up now, because I'm babbling."

"'Kay."

I poke him. "Hey! If you weren't in pain, I'd hit you."

"Lucky ... for ... me ... I ... am." His words are slurred. He closes his eyes again.

I slip out to stretch my legs, circling around the other cars on board; always keeping the truck in sight.

I come back to the truck on the passenger side. Jared's still resting; his head pressed against the seat. I know him so well, but I've never seen him asleep before. I step closer and my heart wrenches.

There are tracks of tears down his cheeks.

I may not totally understand everything he's going through, but he's clearly suffering.

I climb as quietly as I can into the driver's seat, grab the steering wheel at ten and two o'clock and stare straight ahead, jaw clenched, willing the ferry to go faster.

I can't wait to get to the dentist.

The dentist wears a pink shirt and has a bushy moustache and talks to both of us like we're three years old.

"So! What do we have here? Ooh ... a nasty abscess. That must hurt!"

Jared nods faintly.

"Well you're lucky this lovely young lady brought you in. We'll make you good as new, but it's never good to leave these things."

When he speaks to the hygienist, giving her instructions, asking for instruments, he's much calmer, quieter, and I find that reassuring.

I just naturally followed Jared to the room when they called him in and, as soon as he sank into the chair, he reached for my hand. Now that the dentist has his gloves and mask on, I speak up. "I should probably go to the waiting room."

Jared's eyes widen. He shakes his head. "You said ..."

The dentist laughs. "You're not in my way. And if you keep the patient happy, we're glad for you to stay."

So I do. I try to smile at Jared every now and then, without staring into his mouth. While not exactly romantic, it's a bizarrely intimate experience to share.

It doesn't take long, and when it's over the hygienist hands me a pack of gauze and a prescription for antibiotics, while Jared pays the balance not covered by his mom's insurance.

I head back to the ferry dock, coming to full, careful stops. Indicating for every turn. Nursing Jared's precious truck.

"Nice driving." Jared's words are still muffled from the freezing.

"How is it?"

"Much better. No more pain." The part of his mouth that can move, smiles. "Thanks to you."

"I think it's more like thanks to the dentist." But my heart swells. I pull into a parking spot, and tap his phone, lying on the seat next to him. "Text your mom and tell her everything's OK. I'm going into the pharmacy to fill your prescription, and we can get back on the ferry."

It's only as I'm washing my hands in the bathroom on the ferry that I realize I'm tired. And hungry. I shake my hands dry.

Maybe a sandwich at the bakery.

Find the paper towel dispenser empty.

And a lemon square – I've earned one.

Wipe my hands on my shorts, push the door open with my hip, and run straight into Betsy.

"Meg! Doing some shopping on your day off?"

I fall into step beside her and we both head for the door at the end of the aisle. "No, actually. I just got back from the dentist."

"Are you OK?"

"Fine. It wasn't for me. It was Jared. He had a terrible abscess. He could hardly talk." I'm halfway through the door, and Betsy isn't following me. "Betsy?"

She stares at me. "Did you say Jared? As in, he went to the dentist in Kingston with you?"

"Yeeesss." I review my last few sentences in my head. They all seem straightforward. "Why?"

We stop at a spot by the railing.

"Jared doesn't leave the island."

I nod. "Yeah, I hate leaving the island too, but sometimes you just have to."

Betsy lays her hand on my arm. "No, Meg. Listen to me. Jared has not left this island since his dad died. Since the wake, to be exact. It was in Kingston. Then he came back for the funeral, and he hasn't left since."

I laugh. "How is that even possible, Betsy? There are some things you just can't get on the island."

"It's been done before. One woman was banned from the ferry after she jumped off it. Twice." Betsy shakes her head. "Of course, even she got a ride over in a private boat now and then. But, if you think about it, between Jared's mom, and packages getting sent over on the ferry, and the stores in the village, you could manage."

"Unless you got a tooth abscess."

"Well, yes. I don't know any dentists who make house calls."

"And, if you needed a birthday gift for your mother, you could ask a friend and she might get it for you ..."

Betsy claps her hand over her mouth. "Is that how he did it? Jane loves that necklace. She figured he must have ordered it online."

"Why? I mean, are you sure he doesn't go over? Maybe he does, and he just doesn't tell anybody." Even as I say it, I'm remembering the look on the face of the ferry worker when he guided us onto the ferry this morning. Maybe not surprise at me driving. Maybe shock at seeing Jared going to Kingston. He, of all people, would know if Jared takes the ferry.

Betsy's shaking her head. "He doesn't like to talk about it, but once, when his mom pushed him, he said his dad died the last time he left the island, so he prefers to stay."

I replay Lacey's half-statements – "You'd have to go to Kingston, or Ottawa to go to Meg's kind of show," and "It's not the dentist he's afraid of ..." Jared cutting her off both times, warning her to stop talking.

And his mom – what did she say? – "It's not me you have to convince. I'll be more than happy if you can get Jared to the dentist." She wasn't worried he wouldn't go to the dentist, she was afraid he wouldn't get on the ferry.

No way ...

We pass the cottage that, for me, always marks the final approach to the dock. The island is coming up fast ahead of us. "I should go. I'm driving."

Betsy walks as far as her car with me. I pause to hug her. "I'm still kind of in shock about this. It's so hard to believe."

She squeezes me back. "Well, I find it equally hard to believe that after all these months, you took that boy off this island just like that."

I snort. "Well, he was in a weakened state."

"I'm being serious, Meg. He seems to trust you."

Wow. As I walk back to the truck I wonder, is Betsy right? How could she be? It must be a mistake.

But it explains a lot. Jared's tears on the way over to Kingston – they make sense if today was the first time he left this island for nearly a year. Even more so if the last time he went was for his dad's wake.

I hesitate before pulling the door open. Should I ask him about this now? Or when he feels better? Or never?

A noise interrupts my train of thought. A snore, to be exact. I look over to see Jared sound asleep. He's still pale, and the dentist's pushing and pulling has left his lips dry and cracked, but his features are relaxed; there's no pain in them.

I'll see if I can drive off the ferry smoothly enough to avoid waking him.

Chapter Twenty-One

ow is he?

     My sleep is more interrupted than the bad old days at the beginning of the summer.

The last I saw Jared he was semi-conscious and collapsing into his bed. He was still sleeping when I checked on him after riding Salem, and he was still sleeping when his mom came home early from work to keep an eye on him.

How is he now, and how has he been for the last nine months? Never leaving the island? Not once? Not ever?

The pain of a tooth abscess seems like nothing compared to the pain that must have driven that reaction.

I don't need my alarm clock. I'm up super-early. So early, that I run first, then come home, swim, get dressed, then ride my bike up to Jared's and I still have an hour and a half before I have to be at work.

How is he?

Rex meets me on the road, escorts me into the driveway and waits while I lean my bike against the barn.

I scratch his ears. "Hey buddy. I need to see Jared."

The dog's ears tip forward and he runs ahead of me to the kitchen door. He whines and paws at it. *Please let Jared open it.*

"Meg!"

"Hi Mrs. Strickland. Sorry for being here so early …"

My words are cut off by the smushing hug she pulls me into. I hesitate, then circle my arms around her too. Rex leans against our legs, his tail whacking the door frame.

She steps back. "I owe you, Meg. You did something amazing for Jared yesterday."

"Oh, it was really mostly the dentist."

She smiles. "Well, of course, I'm glad his tooth is better, but we both know it was much more than that …"

"OK, come on Mom. Leave her alone." Jared's hand on his mom's shoulder guides her out of the way, and there he is. He's wearing jeans, as usual, and a t-shirt, as always, but he's barefoot. It makes him look vulnerable. His feet, and toes, are long and narrow.

"Are you staring at my feet?"

"Yes, sorry. I might be."

"Why?"

"They're nice."

"Keep her around Jared!" Mrs. Strickland walks by the doorway carrying a coffee mug and a plate. "I'm your mother, and even I don't like your feet."

"Whoops. Sorry. Didn't know she was listening."

He steps out onto the porch with me and pulls the door closed behind him. "Now she's not."

"Good." He grins and I shake my head. "I don't mean 'good' that your mom's not here – I like your mom – I just mean, you look good."

"Better than last time you saw me."

"A little. Although I do find drool very attractive."

"Hey!" He grips my arms. "I wasn't drooling."

"Whatever." He's so close. I could just step forward. I could just lean my head against his chest. I could ...

The kitchen window cranks open a few more inches. "Jared Strickland, you be nice to that girl. You owe her."

"Oh God. My mother. Sorry."

"Like I said, I like her."

He sighs. "She means well. Everybody means well." He lets go of my arms and drops to the top step, pats the wood beside him, and I sink down too. "I'm guessing you heard some things about me yesterday."

My instinct is to deny it, but that would just be stupid. Somebody, somewhere on the island was probably told what sandwich I ordered from the bakery yesterday – even though it was plain old chicken salad; even though they probably didn't care – that's just the way news travels around here. It would be dumb to tell Jared I haven't heard anything. "Betsy mentioned something."

He nods. "If it wasn't her, it would have been my mom, or Doug, from the ferry, or somebody else." He looks off to the fields. "Do you think I'm crazy?"

"Not crazy. But I have to admit, when you said you didn't like to leave the island, I had no idea you meant not at all. Like, literally, not setting foot off the island ..."

Jared's furrowed brow, serious face, make me pause, change tacks. "Maybe you could explain it to me. Then I'm sure I'd understand."

He looks at his watch. *Great. Is this him getting ready to duck out of the rest of the conversation?*

"Have you had breakfast?"

"Um ..."

"Didn't think so." He stands up, gives me a hand, and pulls me to my feet, then leads the way into the kitchen. "Pancakes or waffles? Bacon or sausage?"

"Can you even eat? With your mouth?"

He grabs a spatula. "Are you crazy? I missed a whole day of eating I need to catch up on. Plus, antibiotics are amazing things."

His mom walks in, dressed for work, bag over her arm. "Hey Mom, I'm making Meg pancakes."

She smiles. "Great. Have a good day you two. Bye!"

Jared makes great pancakes. I like my bacon crispy, and he doesn't, so that works out well. Between the two of us, we finish all of it.

Even after yesterday's dental work, he eats faster than me, so I mostly chew, and he talks.

"It wasn't like I planned to not leave the island ever again. I didn't think of it like that."

He spears a piece of pancake. Chews. Swallows.

"It was just the first few times I went to get on the boat after my dad died I thought 'If I hadn't left that last time, he'd still be alive.' And then I'd think 'What if something happens to my mom, or Rod, and I'm not on the island?'" He holds up his hand. "And I know that's not rational thinking, because *they* leave the island, but it wasn't a rational thing. My chest would get tight, and I'd breathe faster, and then, you know how it is; I'd see somebody I knew in line, and they'd pick up whatever I needed over in Kingston ..."

"Mmm-hmm." I raise my eyebrows at him.

"Yes, you're right. I got you do to that for me. But I *so* appreciated it, and you did *such* a good job."

I swallow my mouthful. "Go on."

"And then I just started avoiding it. It's amazing how you really don't *need* to go over if you don't want to."

"But, Jared, nine months?"

He shrugs. "I know. And then people started noticing, and my mom started bugging me, and then I felt like if I *did* get on the ferry everybody would be staring at me."

"Yeah, well instead I got stared at."

"That's 'cause you're hot and the guys who work on the ferry like the look of you."

I wave my fork at him. "Try again."

He shrugs. "That's it. That's my story. Until one day a really bossy girl forced me to go on the ferry."

"Oh, now I see how this story's going to be told in the future."

He laughs. "If the shoe fits."

I glance at the microwave clock, and nearly choke on my bacon. "Crap! I have to get to work!"

He grabs his keys. "I'll drive you. I guess I owe you a lift."

****

He picks me up from work too, because I left my bike at his place this morning.

"So, what's the plan for this afternoon?"

"Jumping."

"Really?"

"Yup, it's about time. Especially if I'm going to give Lacey those lessons she wants."

"Hmmm."

He accelerates as the truck hits the straight stretch of road leading to his house and I have to roll my window up so he'll hear me. "Hmmm, what?"

"Just, I was starting to wonder if jumping for you was a bit like the ferry for me."

I stare at him. "Really?"

He shrugs. "Yeah. I mean, the last time you did it, your horse died. And every time I mentioned showing you kind of ducked the conversation."

"Yeah, well apparently you wanted me to barrel race her."

He shrugs. "Hey, I didn't know you couldn't jump at the shows on the island."

I lean forward. "Well, anyway, you're wrong. I wasn't the one avoiding conversations."

He brakes for the turn into his driveway. "Yes you did. Don't lie." He fake pouts. "I got you this perfectly good horse, and made you a beautiful sand ring, and you don't want to show her."

It's instinct that makes me reach out, and grab at his bottom lip. It's what I do when a horse is standing dozing with his lip hanging down. Except, as I touch the soft skin, Jared jumps, and I remember he's not a horse.

I gasp. "Sorry! Did I hurt you? I shouldn't have done that."

He grabs my wrist, brings it back to his mouth. I'm not sure what to do, so I fan my fingers out with my thumb touching his lips, my pinky cupping the curve of his jaw, and the other fingers spreading across his cheeks. Soft skin. A tiny bit stubbly. Warm.

Warmth shoots through me, too. "Oh ..." It doesn't mean anything. It's just a noise to accompany an exhale. A way to manage the butterflies swarming inside me.

I stare at him, and he stares at me, and I think the more I get to know him, the easier things are between us and, at the exact same time, the more I get to know him, the more tension crackles between us.

Like now. I can practically hear it.

Until Rex barks. And barks, and barks. There's a pick-up truck pulling off the road.

Jared swallows hard. "Rod."

I lower my hand. "And look. Lacey too."

He brushes my hand along the seat, where they can't see it. "OK?"

"OK." I smile. "Lacey seems to have pretty good timing."

"Oh my God!" Lacey picks the burrs out of Salem's tail as I wrap her legs. "I heard you took Jared *off the island*!"

I straighten, smooth the saddle pad over the mare's back. "Well, he didn't have much choice Lace. He was in a lot of pain."

She shakes her head. "I don't think he would have gone for me. Or my dad. Or his mom. We've all begged him. He would have stayed here and suffered. He likes you."

"I don't know Lacey. You wait until you have a tooth abscess and then figure out if you think anything would stop you from going to the dentist." But my insides are warm. *He likes me.* It's amazing to hear somebody else say it.

I pinch the inside of my wrist. *Consider the source.*

OK, true. But it's still nice to hear.

We still haven't picked up Tom's jumps, but, turns out the reason Rod and Lacey showed up was to bring over a couple of the jumps Lacey uses with Cisco. "Or, as I like to call them, the obstacles he uses to time his refusals," Lacey says, and I laugh out loud.

"I'm serious Meg. You should see him. This might be the first time any horse ever jumps over these things."

I warm up while Lacey directs Rod and Jared in setting up the jumps.

My mind never stops. *Heels down, toes in, leg on, seat light, shoulders back, hands quiet. Quiet. Quiet!*

And Salem sends the messages right back to me. *I'm not ready yet. I'm still stiff. I don't want to take your contact. It's hard work.*

I'm tempted to take shortcuts. To jiggle my hands. To trick her into looking pretty, even if she isn't working as hard as she should.

Be patient. I need to work hard if I expect her to. *Use your leg.*

I breathe, letting tension out, gathering oxygen to fuel my muscles. Keep my hands still and gentle. Squeeze her sides. She arches her neck, then hollows it again. Arches her neck again, and her mouth comes alive through the bit and reins.

But is it the real deal? Are we really working, or is one of us cheating? This is where a coach, or at least a mirror, would be handy.

"She looks good. She's tracking up."

"Oh. Thanks Lace."

"Anytime."

We're as ready as we're ever going to be.

Is Jared right about my jumping? Have I been avoiding it on purpose? I let the thought float through my head as I put Salem on a nice, round circle, building her rhythm and establishing her bend.

I don't think so, but there's only one way to find out.

I point Salem at the first jump.

She pitches her ears at it, swings them back to me, and I give her a tiny nudge with my leg and a reassuring, "Go girl" and hold her mouth just enough for support, not enough to get in the way.

Just like on the lunge line, she reaches forward into a canter and, just like on the lunge line, she takes off a stride out. I'm glad I watched her jump before doing it with her myself because, thank goodness, I'm ready. I keep my hands well forward up her neck, and put an exaggerated loop into the reins to keep from catching her mouth on the landing.

My heart leaps with her, and continues racing after the jump.

From excitement, though – and pride – but not fear.

"That was good!" Lacey yells.

"It was great!" I agree.

And it's shown me exactly what we need to work on. Pacing, and smoothness, and accuracy, of course – always accuracy.

But not courage, or heart, which are the things you can't really teach.

Salem's not Major, and that's OK. She's brave, and eager, and smart, and sure-footed.

I may not want to show her, but I sure love schooling her, and that's OK too.

Because, glancing over at Lacey, pink-cheeked, with her hands clasped in front of her, I'm pretty sure I know someone who would like to show this mare.

Chapter Twenty-Two

It's my birthday, but I haven't told anyone here. Not Jared, or Lacey, and I haven't even reminded Carl and Betsy, who've been busy and distracted with the B&B booked solid for ten straight days.

The thing is, I'm perfectly happy. I have everything I need. So why make a big deal about it?

Slate, of course, remembers. I take my cell phone while I hack Salem, and somewhere on our travels it makes a connection. When I get back Slate's name in my inbox makes me smile.

Happy birthday Miss Meg. How's the awkward cowboy? Any birthday kisses?

A noise at the barn door sends me whirling around, shoving the phone in my back pocket. It's just the barn cat though; Jared's working at Rod's today. The text is cute between Slate and me; mortifying if Jared were to read it.

I make myself a whole box of Kraft Dinner for lunch and drown it in ketchup. *Happy Birthday to me!*

Then I take a book to the hammock – one of my favourites; already read and re-read half-a-dozen times – and read it cover-to-cover again.

I turn the last page with a sigh, and realize the breeze has died.

I'm so hot.

Ugh. Really sticky.

I have to get out of this hammock.

I look out to the sparkling river and, on the way, my eye catches the rowboat. That's it. I haven't been out on the water since the beginning of the summer.

I takes less than five minutes to pull everything together, and I'm shoving the light boat out into the bay, and rowing in search of the missing breeze.

It's not in the bay.

The only thing more still than the air, is the water. When it's like this, I can see all the way to the bottom. Long fronds of underwater plants, and fuzzy rocks at the very bottom, and sometimes man-made things, like an old anchor, or a boat propeller.

The only ripples are made by my oars in the water, and the drips that pour off them when I rest.

When I reach the middle of the bay, I row in a slow circle. There are lives going on all around me – in the occasional houses and farms on the land stretching down to the shore, and in the boats way out in the shipping channel – but here, right now, I'm totally alone.

It's time.

I fish around in my back pocket and take out the braid I fetched from my room when I decided to do this.

Should this be hard? It isn't. It's perfect.

It's my birthday, so I'll never forget the date. And it's beautiful, and peaceful. And I'm ready.

I ease the bands off either end and, careful not to overbalance the boat, lean to drop the hairs, one by one, on the surface of the water.

It's so clear they cast shadows.

A tiny fish comes, and nibbles at one, then swims away.

It makes me giggle. "Not very good, huh?"

For several minutes everything stays in place – the remains of Major's braid, and the boat, with me in it – and then with a quick gust, the wind's back. The flat top of the water ripples all around me, and the hairs disappear.

For one second an ache rises in my throat, and I have to blink, two or three times, very quickly.

But there's freedom, too. I don't have to look after that little bundle of hair anymore. My memories are more permanent than that. And this is a good place to remember him.

I've always loved this bay, but hated its name: Round Bay. Like they ran out of imagination, and just picked the easiest name ever.

From now on, to me, it'll be Major Bay.

Forty-five minutes later, after a dunk in Major Bay, I'm climbing the steps to the cottage porch with my hair dripping down my back.

There's a note stuck to the frame of the screen door – Betsy's handwriting on a lined piece of notepaper:

Meg,

I'm sorry to ask on your day off, but something's come up. We need to serve a meal tonight. When you get home can you come to help?

P.S. It's a bit of a fancy meal.

In retrospect, maybe I should have told a few more people about my birthday.

It's been a relaxing day, but standing here now, with the note disintegrating between my wet fingers, something's missing. I don't know what, exactly, but I do know I'm not that happy to be called into work on the day I turn seventeen.

Oh well.

I pull the note off the door, push inside, dump my bag on the floor and have a critical look in the mirror. My hair's actually drying decently – it's curling into that style they call "beach waves," that all the celebrities always seem to be trying for.

It's either clip back a couple of particularly wonky waves, or start from scratch with shampoo and conditioner. I dig around in my underwear drawer for some bobby pins I'm sure I saw there.

And so, clothes. The lace dress has been hung on a hook on one of the rafters ever since the day of the barbeque when I changed out of it so quickly. It's going to stay there. Surely Betsy doesn't want me to look that fancy.

I pull my bag out from under my bed and retrieve a long, black, jersey skirt I still haven't unpacked. It's comfortable and casual, but nicer than shorts and, with a white t-shirt, it will make me look a bit like a waitress.

I come downstairs, do my usual toilet-standing mirror check. Decide I look extremely put-together compared to my normal island look.

I check my phone before I leave. It's weird not to have a message from my parents. My mom's high state of organization means she (or her personal assistant) never forgets a birthday. The last message, though, is Slate's from this morning.

I reply to it: No birthday kisses. No kisses at all. Sorry.

Wow. That sounds kind of pathetic.

Oh well – maybe Betsy will have a really good dessert for the guests tonight, and I can snag a piece.

Happy Birthday to me.

****

Sure enough, when I walk into the kitchen at the B&B, the table's set with matching plates, and cloth napkins, and a bunch of flowers in the middle. Except why the kitchen table, instead of the dining room? I frown, straighten a chair, wonder where everybody is.

"Meg?" Betsy's voice floats down the hall from the living / dining room. Maybe she wants me to help her move the table settings down there.

"Yes?"

"Can you come in here, please?"

"Sure." I start walking. "Do you want me to bring anything? I could use the tray ..."

I stop dead. Shut up. My mom's standing in the doorway to the big room.

"Mom?"

She smiles. "Happy birthday, Meg."

"What? Oh!" I clap my hand over my mouth. Jared and his mom are standing farther back in the room, with Carl and Betsy.

Jared looks – oh my God – I didn't know Jared could look like that. He's wearing shorts – shorts! Long, with big pockets on the sides. And a shirt with a collar. And his hair looks like it's been washed and hasn't dried with a ball cap on it. He looks like a surfer; sun-kissed and fit, if you ignore his white legs. Which I am. *Wow*.

"I'm sorry. I'm completely confused." I shake my head and Betsy saves me.

She steps forward and hugs me. "Everybody wanted to wish you a happy birthday, Meg. Come in. Sit down. We have gifts." She points to a stack of presents by one of the chairs. "And dinner, after."

"You remembered. And you all came. And, Mom, what are you doing here?"

"It's always easy to arrange a meeting in Toronto, Meg. I set one up for tomorrow so I could be here tonight. Your dad sends his love. He's emceeing the big real estate board dinner tonight, otherwise he would have come too."

"This is from both of us." She hands me an envelope so fat I know there's more than just a card in it. I open the flap and shake out a tack shop gift certificate. "Thank you." But there's more. The envelope's still heavy, and rigid. I jiggle it again, and a plaque slides out, engraved "Salem."

I hold the plaque in one hand, cover my mouth with the other. "Oh. It's beautiful."

"It's for her halter."

I blink hard. "Yes. It's perfect."

"You like it?"

The thickness in my throat makes me afraid to speak. So I nod.

Jared speaks up. "I know somebody who can put that on for you."

I breathe. *Thank you Jared.* My voice is calm when I say, "That would be great."

My mom nods. "Yes, thank you. I'll cover the cost, of course."

Betsy and Carl hand me a gift bag containing what must be one of every island souvenir item ever made. A t-shirt with the ferry printed on the front. A baseball cap. A coffee mug. Two different bumper stickers. Jam, and maple syrup, and soap made on the island. I laugh. "This is perfect!"

Jared's gift is also an envelope. I try not to let my hands shake as I open it. I can't believe I have to open my first gift ever from Jared in front of my mom, and his mom.

It's OK, though. It's not embarrassing. It's another gift card – this time to a restaurant in Kingston. One I pointed at when Jared and I were driving to the dentist – told him they serve my favourite pasta. I thought he was in too much pain to listen to my babbling, but I guess I was wrong.

I look up at him. "Really?"

He nods. "Yup. You and me. Whenever you like."

"I like soon."

"Good. I do too."

"My gift is in the kitchen," says Jared's mom, where she reveals a golden-brown lattice-topped pie with cherries bubbling up between the strips of pastry.

It spins me back to a time that was just yesterday, and was forever ago.

I turn to Jared, seated to my right. "I crashed your birthday pie when we first met, and I still haven't gotten you a gift."

"That's because you're a terrible person." He winks, and my heart flips.

I brush my fingers across his, quick and under the table; so nobody else can see. "I feel exactly the same way about you."

I'm stuffed with about four ears of corn, and salad, and fresh bread, and steak from a Strickland cow, and two pieces of cherry pie, when my mom and I walk back to the cottage.

"It's already getting dark earlier." She's right; the sun is at its most spectacular right now – low and fiercely pink just over the horizon – which also means it's just about to slip out of view.

I shudder.

"You OK?"

"Yes, fine."

"Someone walk over your grave?"

I don't want to be reminded how fast the summer's passing by. "Something like that."

The porch boards creak under our steps. My mom stops, leans against the railing, takes a deep breath in, and out. "What a nice night."

"Fantastic. Thank you. I was so surprised."

"Yes, Betsy did a great job of that."

"She did. She's great. The meal was a surprise. But I was also surprised you were here."

"Well, it was important to me."

"And your gift ... I know you didn't think me having Salem was a good idea."

She shifts and sighs. "You know, Meg, by seeing you here, and the things Betsy's told me, and meeting Jared and his mom – the people you choose to have around you – I realize you're a nice person, and a smart person, and you make good decisions, and I should trust you."

"Wow," I say, and this weird thing happens while I say the word. It's a bit like what happened earlier, when I released Major's mane. Something locked inside me opens up, and a piece of tension floats away and I stand a fraction of an inch taller. "Thanks."

She shrugs. "You earned it." Then the corners of her mouth turn up, and she narrows her eyes. "Jared's cute."

I hold my eyes wide. *Don't blink. Don't blush.* "He's really nice. And smart." *And "cute" doesn't touch how Jared looked tonight.*

"Uh-huh. And cute. Even if you won't say it. What did he say to you when he was leaving?"

I shrug. "Nothing." And this time I don't have to fight to keep my face neutral, because it's true. He didn't say anything.

It wasn't anything he said. It was that, right before he stepped into the car with his mom, he reached out and touched my hair, right behind my ear.

Before I could react, or say anything, he winked and held up a strand of dried seaweed.

That was it. That was all. He got into the car and they drove away, honking and waving, and I stood watching with tingles running up and down my body, and my knees threatening to give.

Chapter Twenty-Three

I've barely stepped through Betsy's door in the morning when the phone rings. Betsy holds it out. "It's for you."

I ease my morning collection of eggs into a shallow bowl on the counter and take the phone. "Hello?"

"Hey Meg!"

"Hey Lace. I'm surprised to hear from you so early. Is everything OK? Do you have to cancel our lesson?"

"What?!? No! I was just calling to make sure *you're* OK."

"I am Lace, but if I don't get to work, I won't be done in time to meet you at five, so ..."

"Oh, yes. So. You'd better go. Bye!"

I've taken my first bite of my sandwich when Betsy finds me again. "Phone again." Her smile tells me who it is.

"Lacey Strickland, how may I help you?"

"Oh, hey Meg. Still good?"

"Fine Lace, thanks. What's up?"

"Oh, I was just wondering. What should I wear?"

"Riding clothes, Lacey."

"The thing is, I'm saving up for English boots, but I still only have my Western ones, and I was wondering if they're going to be OK, or if I should try to borrow some other boots from somebody ..."

"Lacey?"

"Yes?"

"It's me. And you. And maybe your dad, and Jared. You can wear what you like as long as it's safe and comfortable."

"I just don't want to do the wrong thing."

"You won't Lace. Now I've gotta eat."

I'm in the yard, swinging my leg over my bike, when Betsy appears in the doorway holding the phone.

"Lacey again?"

She nods.

"Tell her to hang up the phone, and get to Jared's or I'll be there before her."

Betsy smiles. "Will do. Have fun."

"I'll try. If Lacey lets me."

I'm halfway to Jared's when my phone vibrates. *Lacey.* Ignore it.

Except Lacey doesn't have my cell number. After all today's calls, I don't think I'll be giving it to her, either.

Sure enough I've just passed the hydro pole which, for whatever reason, always seems to be a sweet spot for cell service. I stop, pull my phone out of my pocket and see a new-to-me text from Slate.

She sent it yesterday, in response to my "no kissing" answer and it reads: Why not? What are you waiting for? You have lips, right?

I laugh. Touch my lips. *Yeah, I have them.*

My thumb hovers over the screen, and I contemplate typing: And, your point is? but read the time. I'm supposed to meet Lacey in three minutes. There's no way she'll be late. I'd better go.

Lacey insists on grooming and tacking Salem up. "I'm going to ride her, so it's my job."

"She's so excited about this ride." Rod and I watch as she settles the saddle on Salem's back.

"Is this OK, Meg?"

"Perfect. See how you've left her shoulder free to move? That's great."

I turn to Rod. "I know she is. She called me at work three times today. I just hope she isn't going to be disappointed. Jumping is only going to be a small part of what we do today."

"Oh, I wouldn't worry about that. Lacey can focus when she needs to."

I hope Rod's right because I insist on a long, slow warm-up.

"This might seem boring, Lace, but Salem's still green. With her, if you start off right, she'll be great. If you rush her, things don't go so well."

Lacey shrugs. "I'm supposed to learn not to rush either, so that's fine."

A laugh makes me turn to see Rod and Jared leaning on the fence. Rod winks at me. "This'll be good for her."

I make Lacey and Salem walk, then trot, then walk some more. I test Lacey's eye and accuracy using trot poles and pylons. "Circle inside the two pylons ... now outside ... now do a circle with this one at the centre."

I'm impressed. On Salem, Lacey is a different rider. She's smoother, more at ease; she *belongs*. On Cisco, with his round barrel, Lacey's legs flap around like the most rank of short-stirrup riders, but on Salem her legs have a place to go. They lie snug and rock solid just behind the girth.

"You look great on her! Are you ready to jump?"

"Yes! Oh yes, yes, yes!" She takes a deep breath. "But I want to do it right. Talk me through it."

"No problem." I point to the jump we have set as an X on the long side of the ring. "You're going to do this one."

She nods. "Trot in or canter?"

"I'd canter in, if you feel confident with that. A lot of people think trotting in's easier but I find a canter approach smoother."

"OK. Fine with me."

"So, it's no big deal; she can do it in her sleep. You just want a nice pace – a steady rhythm – and you want to look up and beyond the jump. You're not jumping; she is. You're *allowing* her to jump."

"Got it."

"And you've seen how big she jumps. So I want you to find your balance about four strides out, make sure it's rock solid, and grab a hunk of mane just in case. It's better than reefing her in the mouth. Got it?"

I step back, out of the way. "Just do a twenty-metre circle at C and once you've got your pace, head for the jump!"

Lacey and the little mare approach the jump with matching levels of enthusiasm. They're in a beautiful forward flow and, sure enough, Salem rocks back on her hocks and jumps big. It's great to see her from the ground instead of feeling her from on high.

Lacey's eyes stay locked on something far away on the horizon, and her hands hover over Salem's mane, but she's so balanced she doesn't need to make the grab.

"Great job! Ride a canter circle then bring her back to trot and walk."

As she leads Salem out of the ring, Lacey turns to me. "That was so great! When can I have my next lesson, Meg? Can I come tomorrow?"

Jared raps her helmet with his knuckles. "I don't know about that, Lace. Meg and I might be going out for dinner tomorrow night." He turns to me. "Does that work for you?"

"I, uh …" Lacey's listening and Rod's right there too. But Jared doesn't seem to care. *What are you waiting for?* "Tomorrow night is good. Perfect."

I turn to Lacey. "We'll pick another night, Lacey. Now, if she's hot, you can sponge her and let her graze."

She leads Salem away, and Jared, Rod and I follow more slowly.

"Is your mare for sale?" Rod asks.

"Maybe," I say at the exact same time Jared shakes his head and says, "No way."

"Why not?" I ask.

"She's yours. You don't have to sell her. I'll look after her forever for you."

Something inside me melts. It's the combination of the words "look after" and "forever" and "you" all strung so closely together coming out of Jared's mouth. It's easy to pretend he's talking about me, and not the horse.

You have lips, right? I press my palms against my cheeks to try to keep them cool.

"You two talk about it. If you decide to sell her let me know. Lacey seems to be taking this riding seriously, and I reckon she'll kill that little pony of hers with all her jumping and fancy moves."

I think Cisco's more likely to kill Lacey, but I agree he's not the right horse for the kind of riding she wants to do. Instead I ask, "How would you feel about Lacey taking Salem in a show?"

Rod shrugs. "Sure, if she wants to, it would be fine with me. I guess it would be a good chance to see if she really likes it."

I jump up. "I'm going to tell her!"

Rod laughs. "You're as excitable as she is."

"It *is* exciting!" I call over my shoulder as I run over to where Lacey's grazing Salem.

Lacey holds the lead shank out of Salem's way as the mare wanders toward a particularly juicy patch of grass. "What's exciting?"

"Would you ..."

"Yes?"

"Would you, Lacey Strickland, like to ..."

"What? Meg, tell me!"

"Would you like to take Salem in a show?"

Thank goodness Salem's a calm horse, because Lacey's jumping and squealing would send her through the fence otherwise. As it is, the mare turns an ear in our direction, lifts her head and keeps her eye on us for a few seconds, before reaching for a fresh mouthful of grass.

We talk, and plan, and plot, and dream. Once Salem's been turned out, as Lacey's ready to go, I call her into the barn.

"Show me your feet."

"Why? They're huge. I hate them."

"Well, I wouldn't say they're huge. But they're big enough, and mine are ridiculously small, and I'm wondering ..." I disappear into the empty stall that's become my tack room. "If these would fit you."

I hold out my tall black show boots. Not used since the day I crashed on Major. Sent, by my mom, in the box with my saddle. Still shiny, although they'll look better with a polish.

"No. Way. You wouldn't." Lacey claps her hand over her mouth and shakes her head.

"Of course. There's no point in them gathering dust here if you can wear them. Then, if you want to keep showing, you can buy your own."

"Oh, I will. I already know that. I definitely, one hundred per cent, absolutely ..."

"Sit down and let's try them on."

They fit. They're not perfect. My calves are a couple of inches longer than Lacey's, but the boots are broken in, so there's some give around the ankles. "They're going to push against your knees, but they're not really supposed to be super-comfortable. They're supposed to look good." I stand back, tilt my head and narrow my eyes. "And they do look good."

"Thank you so much, Meg."

"My pleasure. There is something you can do for me, though."

"What is it?"

I tell her, and she agrees, and we're both happy as she drives off, talking Rod's ear off about Salem, and showing, and riding boots.

While Jared puts away the equipment he was using earlier today, I tidy up the barn. When I sweep the final pile of dust outside, it's already getting dark.

The summer's passing, that's why. The sun's setting earlier and earlier. *What are you waiting for?*

Slate's words, even though not exactly profound, have stirred me. *You have lips, right?* Jared got me Salem. Jared made my sand ring. Jared took my hand, that day in the rain. Jared's taking me out for dinner.

Maybe it's my turn.

The thought sends butterflies cartwheeling around my stomach. Half of them are big, bold, excited butterflies, the other half are tiny, flitting, and terrified.

I hang the broom in the barn, and stoop to scratch Rex's ears. "I guess, maybe, I do need to get going. What do you think?"

The dog gives me a quick, darting lick, then whines, the noise generated from deep in his core. Jared's walking across the yard in our direction. Rex jumps up, his whole body wagging as he runs to him.

"Hey buddy." Jared reaches down to pat the dog. I'm still crouching, feeling like I might be sick. Because, now that he's here, what next?

Rex breaks away from Jared and runs back to me.

"All done?" Jared steps toward me, reaches out his hand.

I take it, let him pull me up. "Yeah. I just finished sweeping the barn."

"It's getting dark to ride your bike back." Now that I'm up, I wait for him to let go of my hand, but he doesn't. "Do you want me to give you a lift?" We're standing so close that, when Rex tries to walk between us, he doesn't fit.

I whisper. "Maybe not right now."

"What was that? I didn't hear you."

Go. Do it. Now. I reach for his other hand, pull him so near I can feel his body warmth. Put my mouth by his ear. "Can you hear me now?"

Instead of answering, he lets go of both my hands at once and circles me with his arms. Gathers me in, and almost literally sweeps me off my feet, so that I have to stand on my tiptoes to keep from falling over.

We stand breeches against jeans, shirt against shirt and, breath on breath. With our breaths coming faster and faster. And Jared's eyes staring into mine, his lips so close the tiniest pucker of my own lips would reach them.

My whole body responds. I want to wrap my legs around his. I want to reach around to the small of his back and pull him harder up against me. I want to start the kissing, but I also don't want this moment to end because we'll never get it back.

We'll never again be just about to have our first, serious, major, romantic kiss and I don't want to let go of that lightly.

I blink. *Remember this.* He blinks. *Lock this away; seal it up tight. Hold onto it.*

And then one of us – I think it's me – makes a little hiccupping sound, like a catch of breath, or a tiny exclamation of desire, and that breaks the trance, and Jared puts his lips on mine, and I reach my hands up and cup his cheeks, and we kiss, and we kiss, and we kiss. He pushes me backward until I hit the fence, and I hitch myself up on the rail and keep kissing him.

It's Salem who saves us from being caught in the act. She nudges my back and makes me open my eyes and look over Jared's shoulder, which is when I notice the light switched on over the kitchen entrance, and the door opening.

"Your mom," I whisper, and "Shit," Jared mutters but I'm kind of glad she's there because I'm so high on adrenaline and hormones, I need a third party to supervise me, keep me in check. I need someone to force me to take my hands off Jared, because there's no way I could make myself do it.

I pull away, breathing hard, and the thing I feel, stronger than the excitement, and the adrenaline, and the sheer lust crashing through my body is relief. Sweet relief at finally, finally sealing the deal.

"You're great," I whisper in his ear. "That was absolutely great."

Chapter Twenty-Four

I float to work, then fly through my duties. Nothing bothers me. Not the guest who takes a shower with the curtain hanging out of the tub. Not the one who studies Betsy's extensive selection of teabags and asks, "Don't you have any organic, vegan, fair trade, hundred-mile teas?"

It's surprisingly easy to smile and say, "Unfortunately the only tea plantation within a hundred miles went out of business last year."

"That's a shame," says the guest and, out of the corner of my eye, I catch Betsy, hand clapped firmly over her mouth, and shoulders shaking, scooting out of the room.

"You're in a good mood."

"The best."

"Anything you'd care to share with me?"

"Just life. Things. Lacey's going to ride Salem in a show." *My lips still tingle when I think of Jared kissing them.*

"Well, that sounds good for Lacey ... but are you sure that's what's got you so happy?"

I hesitate. I want to tell someone about Jared and me, but I also think of Betsy as a bit of a surrogate grandmother – how much can you really tell your grandmother?

I compromise by telling Betsy, "I'm going out for dinner with Jared tonight," and, a few minutes later, in the murky warmth of the chicken coop, pulling out my phone and thumbing Slate a text: Done. Lips used. Amazing. Perfect. Not sure why I waited so long.

Her answer comes back, short and sweet, before I'm even done sweeping out the coop: Told you so! Good job Megsters.

I've come to love my loft bedroom. During the day, the sun on the roof stokes the heat under the eaves, so that when I come upstairs the air is hot, and dry, and smells like untreated wood. Then, when I go to bed, the night breezes float in, smelling like hay and the river and, sometimes, fresh rain on the fields.

Now, standing in nothing but my underwear, I'm glad of the softness of the warm air on my skin. I reach tall, bend over and touch my toes. *Stretch, bend, breathe.*

This is no big deal. This is fine.

The white lace dress lying across my bed tells me otherwise.

I shrug into it. The dainty cuffs of the three-quarter sleeves look strange against my tanned arms. I don't feel properly dressed with air around my legs, instead of breeches or running lycra.

It'll look good with the cowboy boots I borrowed from Lacey, though. I'm sure of it. Pretty sure, anyway. It *should* look good ... oh God, I just have to put the boots on before I lose my confidence.

The first boot sticks for a minute – *this was a bad idea, it's not going to fit, I should just wear capris and a t-shirt and sandals* – then my foot slides right in.

Perfect fit. I sit on the bed, and stretch my legs out in front of me. Admire my pointed toes. The boots were definitely the missing ingredient.

Go downstairs to the mirror. That's the best way to tell.

It's from my precarious perch on the toilet that I look out the window to see Jared's truck, halfway down the driveway.

Do I have time to change?

I look in the mirror. I look nice. Country casual. Like I made an effort, but not too much.

I'm *not* going to change. I'm going like this.

Still, stepping out on the front porch is more nerve-wracking than riding into a show ring. At least in the ring, I know my job, know I'm wearing the right uniform; know I belong.

Jared gets to the bottom of the stairs as I reach the top. For a minute, neither of us says anything, and then he whistles.

My cheeks are so hot I must look like a tomato. "I didn't know you could whistle like that." Stay calm. Walk down the stairs. *Don't trip.*

He takes my hand at the bottom of the stairs. "I didn't know you could look like this."

"Like what?"

"Like …" He shakes his head. "I don't think I'm smart enough to describe how you look. You look the way I imagine when you're not around, and I close my eyes and think of you."

As he's still talking, before he can even close his mouth, I step forward and kiss him, and while we kiss, I close my eyes and the picture that floats into my head of Jared is amazing.

I open my eyes, step back, look him up and down. "You look just that way too."

I pause with a forkful of pasta halfway to my mouth. "Is this OK?"

Jared smiles. "Of course, it's great."

"I don't mean the food. I mean, being here. On the wrong side of the harbour. With your mom and Rod on the island."

His foot finds mine under the table, and he gives it a nudge. Somehow it's more intimate than holding hands – and doesn't come with the risk of knocking over the tall, skinny water glasses that stand between us.

"You know, Meg, the thing about that is, I just had to realize something."

"Oh, yeah? What did you realize?"

"I realized feeling secure was about being with the right people – the right person – and the fact is, that person is sometimes going to be on this side of the ferry, and I can't let that keep us apart."

Yay! I want to yell it, but he's not done talking.

"Also, I kind of just feel better," he says.

"Better?"

"About me. About everything. About trying new things – or old things I thought I couldn't do anymore. Speaking of which ..."

His features tense. For a minute he turns into that unfamiliar Jared I saw in the barn when I took my mom to meet Salem.

My chest tightens. "What is it?"

"There's something else. Something I hope you'll think is good."

"So, tell me. I like hearing good things."

"Did you hear about the agricultural college?"

I nod. "They funded it, right? At least for one more year. Wait, are you ..."

He picks up where I trail off. "I'm going to try. It's too late for September, but maybe I can go back in January. If it might close, I should get through while it's still around."

I take my chances with the water glasses, grab his hand across the table. "That's not just good; it's great! I'm so excited!"

"Excited for me finishing college?"

"Well that, of course, but have you thought about how much closer it is to the city? We'd be — what — forty-five minutes apart?"

He opens his eyes wide, raises his eyebrows. "You think?"

My heart sinks. One kiss and I'm already making plans for January. Talk about a good way to scare him off.

He puts his hand on top of mine. "I had it figured at more like forty minutes."

On the way back, we stand at the quiet end of the ferry – away from the benches where most people congregate. The hum of the big engine's exhaust cuts us off from everything else happening on the boat.

We talk a bit.

"By the way, nice boots."

"You like them?"

"Where'd you get them?"

"Let's just say Lacey owed me a favour."

We point at the huge sail being lowered on a yacht nearby, the dog barking on the end of a dock on Garden Island, the sun, burning pink and orange, hardly visible over the horizon.

We hold hands, and we kiss.

The light's dim, and there isn't anybody standing near us, and I try my best to keep the kisses short, and sweet, but I figure there's going to be some talk about this – Jared Strickland, not just on the ferry, but kissing a girl, and not just kissing a girl, but kissing one not from the island.

"You must like me to put your reputation on the line like this," I whisper in one of the moments I've pulled my lips away from his, and let them wander close to his ear.

"Oh, I'm happy to go from 'weird loner who won't leave the island' to 'happy boyfriend.'" His return whisper sends tingles running from my ear down my neck, and back up again.

"Did you say 'boyfriend?'"

He doesn't answer – just kisses me – which I take as a yes.

Chapter Twenty-Five

At least twice a week Lacey comes by, and we work on all the things she needs to have down pat for the show. The show, which is now just a few short days away.

We work on Salem's pacing, rhythm and head carriage. We work on quietening Lacey's seat and correcting her piano hands. We work on accuracy for both of them. Lacey needs to give her aids crisply and cleanly, and Salem needs to respond right away.

If they do all that, I'm not even sure they'll win anything, but they'll fit in. They'll be in the ballpark of all the other competitors.

They need to do their absolute best, and then hope for luck on the side – that they both wake up feeling great, that their competitors are riders of similar ability to Lacey, on horses of similar quality to Salem, and, of course, that the judge doesn't mind appaloosas.

They're doing well. Today's been a good schooling session. Jared harrowed the ring this morning, so my challenge to Lacey was to make only the most precise of tracks in the fresh sand. "I want to see perfectly round circles, accurate changes across the diagonal, and an absolutely straight turn down the centre line."

After her first ten minutes in the ring, I come in with my critical eye and have to admit, her circles are even, the diagonal goes straight from K to M, and there are only a couple of wobbles off the centre line.

"And the centre line's hard, Meg, you know it is. Plus, we won't even have to do that at the show."

I raise my eyebrows at her. "Excuse me?"

"What? We won't."

"Tell me why we're working on the centre line."

Lacey holds up her hand, ticks one finger at a time. "Accuracy. Obedience. Straightness. Forward pace – because she'll wobble if we're too slow, um ..." She looks at me.

"Preparation to track right, or left, going back onto the rail?"

"Yup. That too."

"So, given all those things, does it matter that you won't be asked to do this exact exercise on the weekend?"

"No. It's good practice."

"Exactly: now show me some transitions."

We're finishing up when Lacey brings up the thing she just can't leave alone.

"Meg, come on! I can do it. You know I can!"

"Lacey, if I *knew* you could do it, I'd let you do it. It's not as simple as you think."

"Puh-leeeeeze, Meg."

"Lacey, I swear, if you ask again, I'm tempted to pull you from that class right now – just call them up and ask them to cancel the registration, instead of waiting to see on Saturday."

"You *wouldn't!*"

"What wouldn't she do?" Jared strides through the sand, to meet me in the middle. It's hard not to reach out for him when he stops just a foot or so from me.

I speak up before Lacey can. "Lacey wants to jump on the weekend, and I'm not sure if she should."

"But, I can do it, I can, and ..."

I hold up my hand. "So, she's registered in a few flat classes, and one over fences, and I told her we'll see how she does on the day. How things are going. How Salem reacts to everything at the show. The thing is, doing an eight-jump course at a busy show is much different than popping over one or two fences here at home."

"Would it help if we set up a course here first, so you could try it before the weekend?"

Lacey jumps off Salem and runs over to hug Jared. "Oh! Yes! You're the best! That would be awesome! You'll see, Meg ..."

As she leads the mare away, he turns to me. "That OK with you?"

I smile. "Of course. Because guess who's going to be the first one to take Salem over the course?"

****

Jared was right about Tom, and his jumps. He didn't so much want more work out of us, as he didn't want to give us the jumps for nothing.

When we arrive, he scratches his head for a while and admits he can't think of much to have us do right away.

"Well, I'd be happy to be on call when you do need help," I say, and that seems to make up his mind.

"You might as well take those jumps now, then. Help me clear out that old barn, I guess."

"What did I tell you?" Jared backs the truck up close to the barn.

"Whatever. It's a gift horse. Don't look it in the mouth. I know I didn't when somebody gave me a filthy old appaloosa."

Jared lunges for me, but I'm out of the truck before he can catch me. "Come on, Strickland. What's taking you so long? We have jumps to load!"

The jumps are in beautiful shape. "Tom's daughter could hardly have used these before she went away."

Added to the two jumps we already have, it's easy to set up a classic hunter eight-jump course.

"We just need two on each long side, and then two diagonal lines. If Lacey goes in an over-fences course it will be some variation of these lines."

We have them set up by lunchtime. Jared disappears into the kitchen to make sandwiches containing a bizarre, but delicious, selection of items from his mom's fridge, and I fiddle with the jumps.

Pacing them out. Adding ground poles. Checking there are no rocks, or divots.

Jared and I sit on the porch steps, chew on our sandwiches, and watch Salem graze.

He nudges my knee with his. "So, what next?"

"Do you really have to ask?"

"I thought so."

The jumps shape our warm-up. We have to twist and dodge and weave around them. They force us to make our circles small; they require frequent changes of direction.

By the time I gather my reins, and sink my heels just a bit lower in the stirrups, Salem's seen each of these jumps many, many times.

I start small. Just one. On a circle. Not a problem. A pop; barely more than a big canter stride.

Then another; same thing.

Next we try a line. I count strides in my head *five-four-three-two-one* between the two jumps. Perfect.

"Can I do anything?" Jared's watching, which I appreciate. Probably good to have an onlooker the first time I take the mare around a complete course.

"You can put back anything I knock down."

"Well, then my job will be easy."

I wrinkle my nose. "Thanks. But like I told Lacey, it's more complicated than it looks."

More complicated because we've never done this together before. Delicate because I need to lead Salem – give her confidence – without getting in her way. Challenging because, while a very short course, it's still a course, and she might get tired by the end. Difficult because this needs to be a good experience if there's any hope of Lacey taking her around a similar course.

Still, there's only one way to get ready.

I double-check my hand, seat, leg position, straighten my back and ask her for a canter. And we're off.

I do the entire canter circle with my eyes on the first jump, so she'll have no doubt about where we're heading but, even before we're in the air over it, I'm focused on the second jump, and then beyond it, and around the corner to the next line.

I keep my leg pressure steady. *Don't rush! Don't die back! Steady, steady, steady.*

When my brain's not counting the strides between the jumps, it's counting the rhythm of Salem's canter – *one-two-three, one-two-three* – steady, even, consistent.

I hold her back slightly as she heads toward the barn entrance, nudge her forward when we head away. To Jared, watching, it should seem like her pace never changes. That's my goal, anyway.

On the sixth jump, she bobbles, lands on the wrong lead. I'm about to take her back to a trot and ask for the correct lead, when she switches for me. It's an awkward change; slightly clunky, but much better than the transitions I'd have to do otherwise.

"Good girl!" Now, focus on the final line. Eyes up, shoulders back, light contact and she floats over the first jump, easily puts in the five strides to the second one, and is up and over. As we canter a circle to finish off she puts a high arch into her neck.

"She's proud!" I tell Jared.

He puts his thumb up. "It was good! Right? It looked good to me."

I push her forward to a walk and give her a great big pat on both sides of her neck. "It was very good."

He steps into the ring. "And I guess I was completely wrong. You aren't afraid of jumping at all."

I shake my head. "No. Actually, that helped me remember how much I love it. I just don't feel like showing right now. I'm happy to leave that to other people."

"Like Lacey," he says.

"We'll see."

Chapter Twenty-Six

I t's all familiar, and it's all different.

Still a crazy, early morning – the sun just slipping up as we roll onto the ferry in Jared's truck.

Still the anxiety about the mare – scrubbed and braided, and wrapped, and blanketed in the trailer – wondering how she'll travel; how many braids she'll rub out by the time we get to the grounds.

When we arrive, the usual rutted, bumpy five-kilometre-an-hour crawl over a rough-mown field, to park the trailer at the end of a row, with another trailer quickly slotting in beside us.

The last-minute brush run across Salem's shining rump, polish of her gleaming saddle and adjustment of a crooked braid – these are all normal.

It's normal, too, to have to prepare the rider. To tuck in shirt tails, and tie on numbers. To say "breathe" and "calm down" and "there's no rush."

Except, this time, the rider's not me.

Lacey with her big eyes, and red, red cheeks, and non-stop smile, can't stop talking, and won't stand still.

She's literally running in circles. "Lacey!" I grab her arm. "Come with me."

"No, Meg. Salem's not ready and we still need to get water, and I want to ..."

"Jared and your dad can do that. Come with me."

I pull her around the front of the truck, to where she can't see Salem any more. To where it's relatively quiet. "I'm going to braid your hair."

"No way, Meg. It's fine the way it is. It'll look stupid in braids. I'm not ten years old. I have to ..."

I pull the passenger door of Jared's truck open and reach into the glove compartment where I stashed a brush and elastics. "Lacey, lean against the seat." She hesitates.

"It's a deal breaker," I warn. She still wants to jump today, and despite a fairly successful schooling session over fences the other day, I haven't promised her anything. She leans.

I brush her hair, slowly, carefully; working the knots out of the bottom first and moving up to the top.

Her breathing slows.

I divide it into two big sections, parted down the back, and she relaxes further against the seat.

I split the left side in three, and start braiding. "Now, let's talk – calmly – about your classes."

Her voice comes back muffled by Jared's truck seat. "OK. Let's talk."

Now it's me who needs calming.

This show is much bigger than I expected – the trailers keep pouring in – and, when we get there, the warm-up ring's packed. This is the true test for Salem and Lacey. I know they can do everything at home, in our quiet ring, but can they do it here, in strange surroundings with strange horses, and people, and yipping Jack Russell terriers everywhere?

Can I lead them through it?

As a rider, I've known what it's like to have to claim my own riding room in a crowded warm-up ring. But as a coach? Never.

This ring, today, is full of real coaches. Ones I've taken clinics from, and whose riders I've competed against. *Craig.* My breath catches when I see him standing there.

But I have to go. It's not fair to Salem and Lacey if I don't. I straighten my shoulders and stride into the ring as though I've done it a million times before.

Lacey's already been cut off by an older rider on a bigger horse.

"Come on, Lace. Grab a spot on the rail. Now. And take her straight up to a trot. Good. And if someone's in your way yell 'Heads up!' Loudly. Now ride."

I look over at the fence to catch Jared's eye. Give an elaborate shrug, laugh at myself, and then turn back to watching my horse and rider move through their warm-up.

Lacey will kill me if I don't get her over one of the jumps in the ring. I wonder if she knows this is much harder work for me than it is for her.

I step forward to stand by the approach to the jump and yell, "Heads up over the X!"

As Lacey heads for it, doing everything I've told her to – looking up and ahead, keeping a light contact while moving forward – another rider drifts into her space.

"Heads up!" I yell again. "You on the chestnut, heads up!"

The rider on the chestnut moves, Lacey and Salem pop over the jump, and I'm more than happy that we've all survived our warm-up ring experience.

"Good job Lace, you can take her out."

I'm following her out of the ring when somebody taps my shoulder. I spin around.

"I didn't expect to see you here. And bossing my riders around, too." It's Craig.

Is he serious? His eyes are twinkling, white teeth gleaming. *He's not serious.*

I laugh and, without really thinking about it, reach out to hug him. "Nice to see you. I've got to follow my horse, but I'll catch you later."

"I'll be watching," he calls.

When I get out of the ring, Lacey's running up her stirrups, while a familiar girl holds Salem for her. "Slate! I wasn't sure you'd come. I thought you'd be too busy getting ready for university."

"Ah Meg-of-mine, how could I miss your debut as a trainer? And I'm so glad I came; I love this mare. She's adorable!"

Lacey loosens Salem's girth and Slate tugs on one of her braids. "And this rider of yours is adorable, too."

I wait for the back chat as Lacey tells Slate she's not adorable, and to leave her hair alone. Instead she just blushes deep pink and says, "Thanks for holding her," before taking the reins back from Slate.

Slate hooks her arm through mine, and we follow Salem back to the trailer. "Meg, you look fantastic. So tanned."

"Just from the neck up, I'm afraid."

"Well, whatever. It suits you. Now, where's the cowboy?"

"Meg! We found you! We had no idea there would be this many people here. This is exciting, wonderful, overwhelming!" Betsy grabs me in a hug, and Carl stands a pace back, a camera with a massive lens strapped around his neck. Not only did Betsy give me the day off, but she insisted she and Carl would come to watch. My ribs swell at seeing them here.

"Betsy and Carl, I'd like you to meet my friend Slate."

Slate accepts Betsy's hug, and hugs her back. "I love your bag," she says.

Betsy looks at her shoulder bag, as if for the first time, and says, "Oh, thank you."

I know Betsy's carrying that bag because it's big enough for all the treats she's brought along – I watched her slice and wrap brownies yesterday – but now Slate's made her feel good about the way it looks too.

"Sometimes I love you more than you can know Slate."

"Right back at ya, Megsters. Now, I want to meet the cowboy."

Distract her. "Lacey's first class is in the A Ring in twenty minutes, and I should actually go find Jared, so could you possibly ..."

It works. "Don't even ask, Megan-baby. I'm taking these two over there now. Maybe we'll buy a donut on the way."

As they walk away I hear Betsy saying, "Oh, there's no need for that dear. I've brought homemade danishes ..."

I don't have to worry about them. Which makes one thing.

****

"You nervous?" Jared nudges me as I stare at Lacey. I narrow my eyes and focus them like lasers as though I can beam, *Post on the right diagonal,* and *Sit up straight,* and *Smile,* directly into her brain.

"A little." I tear my gaze away from Salem and Lacey. "A lot. A surprising amount. My stomach hurts."

Jared wraps his arms around my middle and pulls me tight against him, which I appreciate, but does nothing for Salem. Lacey is stiff as a board and Salem's responding with mincing sideways steps, and the beginnings of dark, damp patches appearing on her neck.

This is no good. Lacey has to chill. *Smile. Breathe. Count one-two-three.* She catches my eye, just for a minute and I mime an exaggerated exhale.

She blinks, twice, then I see her lips form an "O," shoulders settle back. Salem loosens, mouths the bit, directs her motion forward instead of sideways. *Phew.*

All I can do now is watch.

And it's OK. In fact, it's very good. In fact, by the time Lacey and Salem have obeyed every command more or less right on time, and Lacey's posted on the correct diagonal, and Salem's picked up the correct canter lead, and the only transition that wasn't very crisp was – I'm pretty sure – hidden from the judge by another rider, I'm satisfied with their performance.

It takes me a second, after the announcer reads out, "In fifth place, Bewitched, ridden by Lacey Strickland, owned by Jared Strickland and Meg Traherne," to recognize Salem's show name, but, when I hear our names, my heart jumps, and I whirl around and plant a huge kiss on Jared's lips.

"She did it! They did it!"

He squeezes me. "You did it."

****

Craig finds me as I'm studying the course for Lacey and Salem's jumping class. With them going on to win a fourth, and then a third, in their last two classes, there was no way I could say no to them riding in this class, but I want them to be prepared.

"Hey. That mare you brought is doing well." Lacey and Salem beat two of his riders in our last class.

"Thanks."

"Tell me about her."

The story of me working cattle to trade for her, then her running away, training her over milk cartons, and making our own sand ring bubbles up, but something makes me give a different answer. "She's seven, done some jumping in the past. Very versatile. Willing and a quick learner. As you can see, she's very trustworthy with a younger rider. I think you'll like the way she jumps."

He nods. "And you got her, where?"

"Kingston area."

"Sam Jules' place?"

"No." I smile. "It's great to see you again Craig. I need to talk to my rider about this class."

"Of course. Good to see you too. Good luck."

"Watch them." I say.

"I will."

Jared comes up beside me. "You good? What's up? Why are you staring after that guy?"

"I'm fine. It's nothing." It's nothing and everything. It was great to see Craig, but it was also different. It was the way he talked to me. Like an equal, or at least an adult. While I've been away, things have changed, even the things I didn't know were changing.

"You should come and eat lunch. Betsy's set up a major spread."

"I'll be right there. Just give me two more minutes to study this."

As Lacey trots Salem into the ring, I wonder if Craig's watching. *It doesn't matter. This is about Salem and Lacey.*

They have eight jumps to get over, and Salem will clear them easily if Lacey just stays calm and remembers my number one piece of advice. *Eyes. Use your eyes. Tell Salem where you're going next.*

Lacey trots Salem through a beautiful round circle, and when she asks her for a canter the mare steps onto the correct lead. Then it's a nice light rhythmic approach to the first line and they're up, over, down and *six-five-four-three-two-one* strides and up, over and down the second one.

First line done. Both jumps still standing. Salem cantering through the corner on the correct lead. So far, so good.

The second line goes much the same way. So those are the two diagonals done; now they have to do each of the long sides.

The next line has them jumping away from the gate. Salem may never have been here before but, like all horses, she already has the location of the gate seared into her mind. The gate means home.

The gate means "you're done." Now, as they canter past it – past Jared and me standing by it – hesitation sweeps through her. Her ears flick forward and back. She bobbles.

No, no, no don't break. This is a hunter event so they're judged on their smooth flow; their appearance. They're judged on making everything look simple and easy, even when it's not.

Lacey's nudges Salem's side but it's not enough. She's on the verge of dropping to a trot, and I'm shifting from foot to foot, thinking *get after her*, and *go for it*, and *make it happen*!

Yelling isn't really an option. It's not done, and it's just as likely to distract Lacey as motivate her. My frustration comes out in a growl instead. I grit my teeth and crinkle my nose and *grrrrr*.

I don't know if it's Lacey or Salem who hears me, but the mare's ears flick back, then forward, and energy sweeps back into her.

All Lacey has to do is channel it. They finish the corner, and head for the line, which Salem takes beautifully, all long strides and exaggerated bascules in mid-air.

It's enough. I'm satisfied. All I wanted was for them not to have a bad experience in their first over-fences class; this was beyond my expectations. And it's enough for the judges too. They're called in for sixth.

Lacey can hardly believe it. I have to shoo her to ride in and collect her pale pink ribbon.

And once again I get to hear my name, linked with Jared's, read as Salem's co-owners. It has a nice ring to it.

****

Lacey's giving Salem a break, saddle off, in the shade. Betsy, Carl, Rod and Jared have set up a full-on tea party in a quiet corner, and I'm with Slate, watching the last class before they call the division results.

"Look. Over there." I follow Slate's pointing finger to a familiar tall, grey horse.

"Obsidian!"

She nods. "Isn't his new rider cute?" Her braids bounce on her back as she rises in her trot, then takes Obsidian up to a smooth canter.

"And talented, too. He's going well for her. They look great."

We watch in silence as the pair goes around the course. Quiet, confident, making it look easy. The girl smiles the whole way, and I don't think she's faking it.

They exit the ring and Slate sighs. "There goes my childhood."

I put my arm around her. "I know. It's mostly a happy story, though. We all need to move on."

"Speaking of moving on, let's *finally* talk about Jared. He's an eleven-out-of-ten Meg-o. Tell me how he kisses."

"I have a better idea."

"What's that?"

"Look at these results with me and tell me if you think Lacey might be in line for Reserve Champion."

She looks at the paper in my hand, looks at me, and her eyes open wide. "Oh super-wow Miss Meg. I think you just might be right." She grabs me in a hug. "Who knew you'd turn out to be coach of the year?"

My voice is muffled against her shoulder. "I'm not positive. I could be wrong. Let's wait and see."

But I'm right. Even without winning a class, Lacey and Salem's results were consistent enough to beat all but one other horse-rider combination. Lacey's face looks in danger of splitting in two as she accepts her super-sized blue-white-yellow ribbon.

As we watch the girl who took Champion receive her ribbon, Slate whispers in my ear, "Her parents paid big bucks for that horse, and had him shipped in from Virginia. You guys almost beat her on a cow horse."

"Who has a cow horse?" Craig's come up behind us, spread his arms around both our shoulders.

"My new roommate at university. I just got her info yesterday." Slate winks at me, turns a gleaming smile on Craig. "Listen, I'll let you two catch up. I'm going to go meet our little Champion."

"You were right about her jumping, Meg," Craig says.

I nod. "I told you. She was a real find. And she's been great to work with. Super-trainable."

"I have a couple of families who'd be interested in a mare like that. Or, she'd make a great addition to our school. Is she sound?"

"Completely." I catch sight of Rod as he steps forward to congratulate Lacey. "But she's not really for sale."

"Is that so? What are you going to do with her once the summer's over? Bring her back here? You might as well sell her to me, and you can still ride her once you're back."

I grab Jared, pull him over. "Craig, this is Jared Strickland. He's Salem's co-owner. I'm afraid you'd have to work hard to convince Jared to sell Salem to you."

Craig reaches out for Jared's hand and, as they shake, says, "Well, Jared hasn't heard what I'm offering. If she were to vet check sound, and subject to a trial period ..." the figure he mentions is twice as much as I would ever have dreamed of asking for her.

I suck air through my nostrils, stand as straight as I can. *Holy crap!* Jared doesn't even try to disguise his shock. "Really? That much? Oh my God, Meg; you never said."

Rod's standing beside us now. Rod's surprise at the amount is as clear as Jared's. His brows furrow.

"That's because she's not on the open market." I smile at Craig. "I appreciate your faith in the mare, and what we've done with her, but Lacey – her rider – has worked hard with her, and helped make her worth what she is. Jared and I want Salem and Lacey to have a chance to stay together."

I reach out to touch Rod's arm. "Your offer's great Craig, but we've already been talking to Lacey's dad about Salem, so I don't think it's going to happen."

Craig shrugs. "Well, let me know if anything changes. Great work Meg." And with that, he's gone.

Rod and Jared stare at me. "What? It wasn't a lie – we *were* all talking about Rod buying Salem. That one time. Remember?"

Rod blows his breath out. "Hey, I love my daughter, but not for that figure we weren't."

I laugh. "Well, let's just say that's the starting price, and once we deduct the training and showing fees I owe Lacey, that cuts it in half."

Rod narrows his eyes. "Why do I get the feeling that's not exactly how these things work?"

I link my arm through Jared's. "They work the way we want them to work, right partner?"

Instead of answering, Jared swings me out of the way as Lacey comes belting past us to her dad, and throws her arms around his waist. "Did you see? Can you believe it? We won! We won!"

Rod looks over her head and mouths, 'Thank you.'

I give him a thumbs up. "Our pleasure."

Chapter Twenty-Seven

We turn out of the driveway quickly enough, but Jared pulls over less than a hundred metres down the road.

"What are you …"

He leans across me, pushes my door open. "Shh. Just come with me."

"Where …"

"Just come."

I follow him to the back of the truck, climb onto the tailgate beside him.

"Look." We're parked right at a small break in the lilac bushes, and straight through the opening I can see Lacey's barn; Salem's new paddock.

"Oh …"

We left Lacey grooming Salem in the barn and now, as we watch, Lacey leads her out and to the paddock.

At the gate Lacey pats Salem's neck, slips her a carrot – I can tell by the way the mare dips her head and noses Lacey's hand – then pulls Salem's halter off.

Salem stands perfectly still for a minute. She's backlit by the setting sun.

"So pretty," I breathe. Jared bumps his shoulder against mine.

Then Cisco, cheeky little troublemaking Cisco, noses up beside my old mare – Lacey's new mare – and nudges her neck.

Salem hesitates for one more minute, and in that minute she must bunch every muscle in her body, because she explodes in a kicking, head-shaking, arched-neck run, with Cisco galloping to catch up to her.

She looks so happy. So carefree. I'm swamped with love for her.

"You OK?"

My tears are there – not at the surface, but deeper down – and they're not tears of sadness. I concentrate on holding them down. "Fine. Good. I have everything I want, so why shouldn't Lacey?"

"You have *everything* you want?" Jared turns to me, one eye closed against the glare of the early evening sun warming our faces.

I scooch my hand over, lift my pinky finger to tap his hand. "Yup, everything … for the time being."

So, I wish I wasn't leaving here in ten short days.

And, I wish Jared and I weren't going to be two-hundred kilometres, and a ferry ride apart.

It would be good if Slate was going to university just a little bit closer.

And, so I'm still not sure exactly what's going to happen with my riding back in Ottawa.

But.

I trained a horse, and now I know I can train another one and, because I'm good at it, I can take my pick of places to ride.

And I made friends – lots of friends – on the island, which will be great when I come back next summer to work for Betsy and Carl again.

And Jared. Two hundred kilometres don't matter. The ferry doesn't matter – at least not now that he's not afraid to take it. We'll visit each other through the fall, and maybe he'll even be closer in the winter, and the spring. We have next summer to look forward to.

"Are you absolutely positive you have everything you want?" Jared hops down to stand in front of me.

"Um ..."

He digs into his back pocket, pulls out a small pouch. It's so familiar – I've seen a pouch like that before ...

Click. I know where it's from. Which means I know what it is.

"No!"

"What's that?"

"No, I don't have everything I want. I want what you're holding!"

"Are you sure?"

"Positive." I hold out my hands and he places the velvety sachet in them. "Oh, oh, oh ..." I fumble with the string, fish my fingers inside, and the silver chain I pull out catches the last of the sun's rays.

"I love it." I find the tiny, perfect, leaf on the end and press it tight against my breastbone, where it feels just perfect; where it will stay from now on.

I look him straight in the eye. "I love you."

I should be nervous, holding my breath, gripping the tailgate hard enough to break my fingernails.

But the late summer breeze is still warm, and the birds are singing, and, in the distance Salem has settled down to graze in lockstep with Cisco.

And I know what Jared's going to say.

"That's good news, because I love you, too."

About the Author

Tudor Robins is the author of books that move – she wants to move your heart, mind, and pulse with her writing. Tudor lives in Ottawa, Ontario, and when she's not writing she loves horseback riding, downhill skiing, and running.

She's also written:

Objects in Mirror

*Wednesday Riders (*the second book in the Island Trilogy*)*

*Hide & Seek (*a stand-alone short story*)*

If you'd like to be automatically notified of Tudor's new releases, please sign up at: http://tudorrobins.ca/newsletter-signup/.

Word-of-mouth recommendations from readers like you allow Tudor to sell her books and keep writing. If you enjoyed this book, please consider leaving a review on Amazon or Goodreads. Even just a few words really help. Your support is greatly appreciated!

Say Hi!

I love hearing from my readers. You can connect with me through my website – www.tudorrobins.ca – find me on Facebook or Twitter, or email me directly: tudor@tudorrobins.ca.

ACKNOWLEDGMENTS:

Many people provided advice, encouragement, support and motivation in the writing of this book. While explaining what each person did would require another book, I do want to acknowledge the contributions of some specific people by naming them here:

Beth and Greg Caldwell, Veronica Grajewski / Partridge Acres, Sandra Gulland, Margaret Kirkpatrick, Janet Leak, Hilary McMahon, Courtney Mellor, Jason and Christina Pyke, Tim Robins, Evan and Bryn Robins, Patricia Sanford, Kellie Sheridan, The Trillium Hunter Jumper Association, Chris Van Hakes.

I also want to thank every friend, acquaintance, and family member who encouraged me to indulge my entrepreneurial spirit and self-publish this book.

Huge thanks also go out to each and every reader. When you buy my book, or take it out of the library, or lend it to your best friend, I am so happy, and when you write to me, I'm over the moon. Thanks for your support!

Please enjoy an excerpt from

Objects in Mirror

Purchase it in print from Amazon,
or as a Kobo eBook.

Objects in Mirror

I've looked up to Matt for so long. Over the past several days I've also come to like Matt as a person; not just as some abstract riding hero. I trust Matt. And, I have to admit, sitting here next to him in his battered jeans and his faded t-shirt, I think Matt is drop-dead gorgeous.

You and every other girl who's ever met him. I know, I know. It's not hard to think of about a million reasons Matt would never like me. Or at least ten:

First five – Matt:

- Amazing dark eyes;
- Just the right amount of freckles;
- Rides like a god;
- Is nice, smart, funny and everybody likes him;
- Not interested in me anyway.

Second five – me:

- Way too many freckles;
- Much room for improvement with regards to riding;
- Am rarely funny and, when I am, usually end up insulting someone by mistake;

- Am either too fat (my opinion) or too skinny (opinion of assorted adults) – either way body clearly leaves much to be desired;
- Not interested in him anyway. Really. *Not.*

So, considering all the above, I'm pretty curious when he pulls off the bumpy dirt road we're traveling on to turn onto another, even bumpier and much narrower lane which dwindles to nothing by a huge tree growing beside an old fence.

He turns off the engine.

Quiet. Quiet. The quiet's unbelievable. For about 15 seconds anyway and then the first tentative birdsong creeps back in. A cricket starts humming. The landscape, and the wild things that inhabit it, shift back into business; absorbing Matt and me and his pick-up truck into the movements and noises of the summer afternoon.

"There's something I want to show you," Matt says.

"OK."

"This way." He hops out of the cab. We're stopped on a slight angle so I'm pushing uphill as I creak the heavy passenger door away from me. The drop to the ground is higher than I expected and a nettle stings my skin on the way down.

"You OK?" he asks.

"Uh-huh." Stacking hay in the loft, helping repair jumps and, of course, crawling around on my hands and knees with Jamie, ensure my legs are always a mess of scratches, bumps and bruises. The nettle sting just adds to the overall effect.

When I reach his side Matt is balanced on the top rail of an old wooden fence. "It's out there," he says. What I see is a hay field, not yet cut, neck deep in places and swaying in the breeze.

Of course it's beautiful in the way everything unspoiled in the country is beautiful but it appears to be a hayfield like many others I've seen – very much like the ones surrounding both my house and the barn. It's with an equal mixture of interest and uncertainty that I follow Matt up over the fence and jump, feet first, into the depth of the grasses.

I was wrong. I was so, so wrong. There's nothing ordinary about this field. I can't believe how long I've lived alongside fields like this one without ever stepping into one before.

Pushing through the rustling grasses is like swimming in greenery. I lean forward into the wind, barely feeling my feet and legs supporting me, using my arms to part the way and propel me forward.

The field around me is dizzying, like the disorientation I've felt in the ocean when waves dance and ripple all around, and the sand beneath my feet shifts under my eyes. My progress through the field, half surfing, half wading, with the grasses brushing my bare skin has made my whole face smile. When Matt turns to me the same smile is on his lips, pushing up through his cheeks and into his eyes.

He motions to me to stop and rests his hands on my shoulders and turns me, ever so slowly, in a complete circle. We're in the centre of the field, on what must be a slight rise, because all around us that moving, living, dancing carpet spirals out and out until, on all four sides, it hits trees. Not a road or a fence or a building of any sort – not even the truck – is visible from here.

I think of all those times I've heard of places referred to as "the centre of the universe" For me, this might just be it.

Matt leans in closely, cupping his hand around my ear to be heard over the wind-driven rush of the grasses and the exclamations of birdsong. "Amazing, isn't it?"

"Amazing!"

I'm not sure if he can hear me but he clearly understands. He gives me a thumbs-up and a pleased smile and something inside me breaks away and dissolves. A piece of armour I had no idea I possessed is gone; melted in an instant by one simple instance of delight.

I look at Matt in a whole new way now. Smart, still, yes. Talented, of course. Good-looking, especially here in the sun and the wind. But a gift-giver too, kind and generous.

"Thanks!" I yell and the wind whips my word away and scatters it across the field.

82429065R00148

Made in the USA
Columbia, SC
01 December 2017